I0580949

Ghosts Caught On Film

The stories in this collection were previously published in the following publications: "Ghosts Caught on Film" in *Salt Hill*; "New Careers in Science" in *Meridian*; "Pictures from the Coast of France" in *PANK*; "But I Can Only Do it Once" in *The Minnesota Review;* "Caltrops" in *Camera Obscura*; "Embryology" in *The Adirondack Review*; "Origin Story" in *Mid-American Review*; "Hands Like Birds on Strings" in *Bayou*; "You Must Give of Yourself" in *Michigan Quarterly Review*; "Replay" in *Hotel Amerika*; "Heavy Petting" in *The Saturday Evening Post*; "Snuff Film" in *The Shanghai Literary Review*; "The Echoless" in *Hoxie Gorge Review*.

Published by Bridge Eight Press
Jacksonville, Florida

www.bridgeeight.com

ISBN 9781732366787
EISBN 9781087887487
LCCN 2022931244

Printed in the USA
Distributed by Ingram
Cover & book design by Caleb Sarvis

When you're a boy,
other boys check you out,
you get a girl:
these are your favorite things
when you're a boy.

—David Bowie, "Boys Keep Swinging"

Stories

Ghosts Caught on Film

Barrett Bowlin

New Careers in Science

"We can save ourselves," my grandson bellows, holding up a yellowing lipoma the size of shoulder meat, "by understanding what kills us." Here, at the incinerator behind St. Bartholomew's Hospital, my grandson's hair stands on end in the places he's forgotten to apply styling gel. Somewhere in the basement near Radiology is a photograph of my Vance at age seven, dancing shirtless with a burning marshmallow around a campfire. Behind him now, a quick tympani of pressure booms out from where the incinerator sits, next to the hospital's oversized garbage bins. While the huge machine thuds in the nighttime, and while Vance lectures us about the importance of correct diagnosis when we pull shifts in the Pathology lab, we look across the quick dips of land around Bristol and watch as lightning streaks across the horizon around Rhode Island, as bolts spark gently over capsized sailboats in Narragansett Bay and its mangled bridges. Where cars have been left to rust, plastic has dripped from their insides to the ground below, mixing in with the vulcanized rubber of the tires.

"But we can also learn from the dead," Vance says over the hum of the incinerator. There are three of us in his audience.

The two other indoctrinated Pathology assistants—a teenager we picked up from the emergency shelter a few days ago and her mother, forty-something and five months' pregnant—turn away from the heat once Vance, the only pathologist left in our state, opens the door to the fire behind him. I stare through the warmth of the incinerator's open door on my eyelids and corneas. I watch as Vance turns the ball of tissue over in his hands, looking through the clear plastic. He takes a step toward the teenager. She's holding her cellular phone even though we haven't had reception since the last of the storms.

"Biohazard waste comes in red bags. Lab samples this size come in clear bags," he says, stopping and glaring toward the girl and her pink phone. "I know if this is superficial or intramuscular," says Vance, holding the bag closer to the girl's face. "Do you?"

The teenager is trying to sound less unsure. "No," she says, "but I feel hungry now."

I laugh at the girl. Her mother, patting her belly, looks back at me and smiles to be polite.

"Study what you remove from your patients," Vance barks as we finish our rounds outside. He throws the bag of tissue, blood, and fluid into the incinerator, shutting the door behind him. The fire grows in a place just below where we can all see. "Don't just dissect it in the lab," he continues. "Spend time with it before it's burned."

And we disperse back into St. Bartholomew's, through the ER doors lined with makeshift-rubber pads and toward the elevators that will take us up to Pathology. There are burn marks from random lightning strikes along the exterior walls where ambulances used to haul in bleeding and unconscious patients. Throughout the long days of storms, in weather that should have involved a blend of rain and wind, all we received were burn victims. Out past the safe places we've mapped so far around Bristol's harbors, in thin peninsulas and alongside beaches where fog rolls in, thick with static electricity, occasional drifters will stumble up the hill into St. Bartholomew's parking lot, their skin raw from the burns that have lit one side of their bodies up before finally ripping into the ground. More than likely, they'll see Vance as they're nursed back to health. If they perish, Vance will definitely see them, their tissues and organs being salvaged if possible. He tells me he rarely does autopsies anymore, not like he did those first couple of weeks.

As Vance, the girl, her mother, and I walk inside the hospital tonight, I see a few remnant glass shards from where someone forgot to pick up all the shattered and melted pieces from last week's rolling fog of ball lightning. As we pad through the corridors of the ground floor, the pregnant mother and her daughter stop to sit on a filthy gurney while Vance and I wait for the elevator. I can hear the mother's stomach churning—Vance calls this 'peristaltic action'—and I point the woman and her daughter toward the broken vending machine near the CCU and hand them quarters from my pockets.

When I was much younger, I dreamed retirement would involve a bakery. My husband, Vance's grandfather, and I would punch out ovens of monkey bread: Bundt pans of hot biscuit dough, all lined and baked in drizzled masonries of cinnamon, sugar, and butter. Warm and sweet banana slices would be served on the side with black coffee. We would tally the books, fry up bacon, and smoke marijuana after our shifts. I had told him this explicitly. We would buy clear plastic baggies of pot from our grandchildren's shadier friends, and we would welcome glaucoma as easily as we would liver spots, crow's feet, and arthritis.

Later, when Vance's grandfather died while we were getting quotes from banks and contractors, retirement involved a cruise to the Caribbean, the plans made two years in advance, with a group of people I saw only in bowling shirts down at the lanes. I would drift around Jamaica and Bermuda with septuagenarians, some still together after decades of marriage, others alone, like me, their houses needing warmth more so than their hearts. Three months into widowhood, a veteran with a semi-functioning hip asked me out on a date to his gun club. He'd leaned in close and said, "I'll let you fire my .38." And then he had winked and started up a new frame.

When Vance came to get me from the emergency shelter, I think I welcomed a new retirement that would involve the soft mysteries of lab work. It's only every so often that I receive a yeast specimen to stain, but I still smile each time and daydream of Bundt pans.

A wet lasagna of abnormal tissue—Vance calls this a 'neoplasm'—comes in early the next morning, roughly an hour after it's been excised from a colectomy patient three floors up. By this point, blood vessels will have been refitted, two portions of a colon will meet for the first time, and, fingers crossed, blood and mucus will be pumping smoothly and correctly to keep the surrounding tissue alive and mostly unaffected. But the sample the three doctors have sent down is still a map of ham-colored folds with two polyps and a neoplasm the size of a land mass.

I stare at the courier, a babyish man in his twenties who's

scrawled the name 'Sheffield' onto a conference-grade sticky badge he wears over his left shirt pocket. By the looks of his pale skin and the limpid veins running below the dermis, I imagine he didn't see much of the outdoors even before we were warned of potential areas of static charge and surprise storms. He has a wen on his neck that's filled with spongy tissue discharge and fluid. I want Vance to show me how to dissect it.

"This is from Dr. Stenner," Sheffield says. "He says he'll be down for lunch in a bit."

I let Sheffield leave with a nod. Later, Vance tells me—so much like his grandfather—over the lunch of MRE chicken stew that they know it's a good prognosis after GI surgery if the patient begins to fart. Vance says this word in a whisper while reconstituting his soup: 'fart.'

He looks tired, my Vance. He's busy each day with a dermatologist in the operating theater, holding back fat flaps and wiping away sweat from the forehead of one of the two surgeons still living at St. Bartholomew's. He tells me it's like career musical chairs up there: one day an ophthalmologist is trying his very best to repair the sinoatrial node of a hydroelectric engineer we've kidnapped from Delaware. Another day the pulmonologist begins to gag as he saws into the temporal bone of a computer technician's daughter, stifling back nervous sobs as he remembers that we need the technician to reconfigure our LANs and troubleshoot the PET scan system in the basement. Even Vance, who spent years as an intern and resident, always on call and up all hours of the night, working to finally get to a point in his career where a day on the job meant showing up at 9 a.m. and leaving by 5 p.m.—even my Vance is pulling double and triple shifts on top of teaching several of us about pathology, about the strictly vital information he received in this field from medical school and from the hospitals in which he interned.

He reminds me so much of my husband. He parts his hair the same way, gels it down and across his temples, left to right.

Back at the slab of red and gray and pink turkey burger in the Pathology lab, I begin to miss television.

The weather girl's face first went to black as they were about to show me my local radar for Portsmouth: a splash of blues and greens all pockmarked with intense centers of red and orange with yellow halos off the coast. After a day at the commissary and the post office to mail my Vance a care package of caramels and the business card of my salon friend's daughter, I'd just put my feet up when the breaking news music thundered on the TV.

There was excitement in the forecaster's voice. She was saying what anyone with a window could say: *There are storms coming. Stay indoors. Move away from windows. Determine if you are living in a domicile below the calculated tide level and evacuate if necessary.* Her hair was perfect; it was high and feathered like mine was back in the '70s, and I remember thinking that the hair of any weather forecaster wasn't likely to change over the course of a viewer's lifetime. But in that same lifetime, it was doubtful if a person would ever see this many storms coalescing at once: swaths of hurricanes off the coasts of Florida, Texas, and the rest of the southeast; blankets of fog along the eastern seaboard; windstorms from the original 13 colonies that ripped through the Midwest; and everywhere lightning. In Rhode Island, we were consistent about checking for hurricanes and high winds, with an eye on the rickety boat every resident would tie up to a tree in the backyard. By themselves, they weren't much beyond news stories. Together, it was a big, entertaining mess. And I was still on the couch, my feet up and comfortable and warm below two quilts, and I was looking at an old photograph of Vance's grandfather.

When I told Vance about this, he asked if I had my couch up on those special coasters, the ones with the rubber inserts for extra comfort and support.

I had.

He asked if my couch was a sleeper sofa, riddled inside with metal, or if it was just wood, upholstery, and the occasional staple.

"It wasn't a sleeper," I said. "It isn't." And I couldn't help but think about the needlework next to the couch.

When the babyish courier, Sheffield, comes back the next day, the one with the cyst on his neck, I can't help but touch the patch of skin where I had a mole removed last year. A plump nurse in puppy-dog scrubs had toddled into the room with a petite canister of liquid nitrogen. She smiled as she sprayed the mole into a tiny, painful blister. The clumps of the dark skin above it grew brittle and flaked away after several days. I remember that the visit to my own dermatologist the week before had been to schedule a biopsy of the tissue. For a full week, I wondered if it was benign or malignant, if I had more spots on my body that I couldn't see, and if this would mean a short lifetime of chemo-therapy and headscarves or just being more careful out in the sun. Like I imagine Sheffield would have lived, I began to spend less time in my garden. I began to look up to the clouds for sparks or flashes, to see if it was safe to fetch the paper each morning.

"Dr. Stenner says to run an ELISA on this?" Sheffield says, handing me a tube of serum. I look at the sample and see that a patient's name has been blackened out by a pen, and that a number has been written on the side instead.

"HIV?" I ask him. I think about how much my Vance has taught me over the last few weeks. Many patients' samples will be coded in numbers alone if they're to be checked for STDs. Sheffield's cyst seems to have gotten bigger since yesterday. I notice the hair sticking out of it now and wonder if I'd just missed it before.

He nods and shrugs, thanks me, and lumbers out of the laboratory. While I have other samples to process, I always make a place for Vance's specimens at the front of the line, and I start my wash of a fresh microtiter plate in the corner.

Later, while waiting for the sample to react and start glowing—Vance calls this fluorescence—I look over at the blender we use to break down the bulkier samples that come in for western blots. I remember how, when we first came here from the emergency shelter, Vance showed me how to cut up a chunk of a cow's spinal cord. Before we ate steak that night from farther inland—our first fresh meal in weeks—I remember that Vance had told me that we had to check for mad cow disease. He had called it 'BSE.' He smiled as he opened the top to a new bottle of A1 sauce, gingerly pouring a tablespoon's worth on my plate. I remember being so proud of him. I remember the medium-rare pull of muscle between my incisors and canines that night.

Since then, we've survived off the industrial-sized cans of tomatoes, corn, and chocolate sauce stored up in the hospital's kitchen. When we first dared to venture over to the naval base back in Newport, we found the inlet mostly empty. While their kitchens were stocked better than our own, it was the trove of MREs that made the day seem special, with so many different flavors and combinations. The pregnant Pathology student's baby even seems to enjoy the chicken burrito packet. The woman herself, though, says she suffers from indigestion and heartburn.

We're working for the future, I tell her, her teenage daughter distracted all the while, still glancing down at her watch occasionally, still clutching to her cellular phone at times.

After I print out the ELISAs—all negative, the patient clean—I decide to search out Vance. When I pass the doors to the ICU downstairs, a high schooler with ravenous acne whispers out to me from behind one of the tiny rooms' drawn curtains.

"Hello?" he asks. I pull back the curtain farther, and I can see the boy's shoulder propped up, the Lichtenburg burn pattern racing down under the covers near an IV line. For a few days after a burn as light as this one, in these instances where the lightning victim is still around to tell his story, a pattern of red discoloration washes over the skin in ferns and fractals from the origin site.

"Have you seen your chest yet?" I ask. "Have you seen it in a mirror?"

The boy gets up and pulls off his hospital gown. His arms are thin and long and emaciated. His underwear sags as he wheels along a pole with a Lactated Ringer's drip attached, and I can see his skin is pulled tight over his ribs. He stands with his chest to the mirror near the rear wall of his room, with his head arched back as far as it can stretch.

It's not until he turns like this that I see the gauze strips that blanket his back and the anterior of his left thigh. I start adding percentages from the Rule of Nines and figure he's well past the 20% mark for all likelihood of a fatal injury. But the flow of the lightning onto his chest is beautiful, like henna ink or a painting left out in the sunlight.

"Cool," he says.

"It's how the electricity dissipated," I tell him. "You would have died if you were touching or standing near anything metal."

With one finger reaching as far it can the boy traces the outline of the burn from his shoulder, up toward his neck where one branch of the electricity thought about going before it died out in a blink.

"Will it stay like that?" he asks. "Like a tattoo?"

I shake my head. "No," I say, "it'll be gone in a couple of days if it's not gone by tonight. You should come up to the board room this evening after dinner if you're feeling up to it. We have a newcomer orientation once a week on Mondays." I think about this. "Only if you're feeling up to it, though."

"It's still cool," he says, playing with the rip of crimson up by his clavicle. "A nurse gave me something earlier for my back. How bad does it look?"

I can't answer. It's not until I gently touch his other shoulder that I know I'll hear him scream when the nurse comes back to debride the large track of skin that's losing fluids and electrolytes at an unstoppable pace, his skin swelling with edema as we make small talk in the tiny rooms of the ICU.

"Mrs. Stenner?" Sheffield asks. He's laid a hand on my shoulder. I'm daydreaming again in the lab, remembering the path the lightning took across the boy's back and the fire he must have been caught in for so much damage to be made. I don't startle until I see the red and raw cyst on the Sheffield's neck again. From what I can tell in the moment I sneak a look, he's plucked the hair from the center. "Dr. Stenner is looking for those serum results," he says.

I resist the urge to squeeze the man's wen between my fingers, like a blueberry. Like a grape. Like a pearl onion in sauce.

When I catch Vance through the glass at the security desk on the fourth floor, his scrubs lie in a heap at his ankles. In the dim room, his left hand is on the shoulder of the teenager with the cell phone and the second shift in the Pathology lab, and he's pulling her hair from behind with his right. He's riding her like a boy on a stick horse, like he did in our front lawn when he was so young.

As I head down the hallway to the barely used sleep center to wait for him, I wonder if the girl is latching onto Vance for the same reason I have: because he's strong. Because he's beautiful in our molding and worn-down hospital. Because he's formidable against so much that has gone wrong in our lives since the first bolt of lightning struck the ground so many weeks ago. His muscles gleam in the bare light of the security area, my grandson all biceps and triceps, all muscle and strength.

I lie down on one of the quiet and segregated observation beds and wonder about how we've all changed, all of us except for Vance. I think about the venture capitalist downstairs who's working as a janitor during the day now, the one who's eager to learn basic emergency medicine to get away from the bins and mops. I think about the former bartender who stays up nights to stare at the heart monitors in the CCU; compared to her old job, she tells me, the hours are the same but not the social life and the music. All that's gone now, she says.

And there are the two nurses who once delivered babies but now draw blood and hand patients urine cups out of habit. They've tried to make friends with the pregnant woman whose daughter has latched onto Vance. They want to feel something familiar again, they tell me.

But there is always Vance, my Vance, who works so hard, who's always worked that hard and even still, there now, with the girl behind the security desk.

Sheffield finds me again sometime in the evening. I've fallen asleep on the observation bed.

"Mrs. Stenner?" he asks, hesitantly. "How did you make it out there? How did you survive?"

"I think it was because I wasn't outside for most of the storms," I tell him. "I wasn't near anything that conducted." I pause for a moment to think about this. "And I stayed inside for so many days afterward, up until Dr. Stenner came for me."

Sheffield nods. He comes over to sit on the edge of the bed. My arthritis begins to pull from my kneecap as his weight forces the mattress to dip.

"They found me in a coma, still passed out on my bean bag," he whispers. "I think I was naked at the time."

I hug Sheffield close to me and hold him because he's scared.

"You should have it removed," I tell him, breathing in the musk of his neck. "It might be malignant."

The night's orientation for newcomers is attended by five people: the teenage girl, looking fresh and secure, her pregnant mother, Vance, myself, and the dehydrated mechanic we found staggering around a few days ago, out past the rainwater barrels and barbed wire.

He's volunteered to outfit St. Bartholomew's remaining ambulance with static-resistant padding if he can just get back to his garage.

"This one?" Vance asks. "Is he saying much now?"

"He does between meals," I tell him. "The girl's tests came back negative, by the way." I sip from my coffee cup. I have a collection of individual coffee packets near my cot in the Pathology lab. "I can run a Pap smear if you bring me a sample," I say.

Vance peers over his shoulder to the teenager and her mother. They're staring at the mechanic, whispering in tones below what the man can hear.

"A boy in the ICU died tonight," Vance says. "I don't know if you met him or not."

"The burn victim?" I ask. "That's horrible. I think I invited him to the orientation tonight."

Vance nods. I want to tell him about the pans of monkey bread and the coffee that would taste so differently from what we're drinking now. I want to confess to him about my dream of smoking pot. The mechanic looks up at the clock and checks his watch. I wonder if it's still working.

"Your friend? Sheffield?" Vance asks. "He traded us a run to Portsmouth for removing that cyst on his neck." He sips at his own coffee. "We should be safe and test it for anything in situ." He sips again and pauses. "I wanted to tell you that I need you here. We all do. I wanted to thank you," Vance says, his head slung down and drooping.

"Well, I need you, too," I tell my grandson, kissing him on his forehead as he bends toward me, "you darling, wonderful boy."

As the mechanic gets up to leave, I stand to do the same.

"Did you see the child's chest?" I ask. Vance nods. "It was so beautiful. There won't be anything to salvage off him, will there?"

I remember the Rule of Nines again, where each burned segment of the body is given a percentage of the total area of exposed skin, a melted and destroyed pattern, all based around multiples of nine. Each arm is given 9%. So are the head and neck together. Each leg makes up 18% of the total body surface area, as does each side of the torso, front and back. That last 1% is calculated when one's genitals are burned, which they frequently are. With each of those little numbers, I think, there's a ribbon of necrotic tissue beneath, a patch where vessels leak fluids and edemas flood and swell.

"No," Vance says. "There's nothing left."

In the tiny refrigerator we use in Pathology for sample storage, someone has left a small, plastic ramekin with a growth of skin the size of a fingertip, still floating in formalin, for me to cut, wash, and wax. Like Vance has shown me so many times before, I chunk up the cyst and plate both into tiny plastic cassettes that I run through baths of ethanol and toluene, chemicals that lyse the tissues into smaller and smaller collections of cells. Each time I dip the cassettes into their own little pools of paraffin for study, I think of the time I visited Madame Tussaud's with Vance's grandfather. We stopped to giggle just a bit at the guillotined heads on stakes from the French Revolution. Whomever had molded Robespierre's poor mask had kept the large boil on his cheek, the one he tended to brush absentmindedly during his speeches. I wonder if the museum is still taking tickets, if the great double-decker buses are still running out front.

After I set the tissues up for western and northern blots, after I make backup samples in case we need them, I remember that I'm supposed to carry the remains of the cyst out to the incinerator. The paraffin will take until morning to set, and there's time to wait for Sheffield's return. Tonight, I'll toss the leftovers of his excised flesh into the fire, and it'll burn as dimly as a yellow lipoma trapped in plastic or an excised mole. Or a tube of rough serum. Or the body of a child trapped in fire.

I look toward Portsmouth but can see only cables and arches of the Mount Hope bridge. I remember that this was one of the local tragedies near the beginning of the storms, how so many were caught under the metal and wires and tons of steel as they tried to escape inland, the lightning coming down in pulses and bursts through the metal and tension rebar under the concrete, and now how we'll occasionally see a flicker of electricity through the fog that lumbers onto and through the bridge lanes. When it does, we try not to think about the bloated and burned, or about the trapped numbers there among the herds of cars and RVs. We instead head back inside, back into St. Bartholomew's fortress of cinder block-lined rooms and closets, back to the warm skin of people we've found since the lightning came.

You Must Give of Yourself

You're a minute into a pair of bisteccas on the grill, chef, right at that point before the char starts to collect on the exteriors, with one eye on the coals and another on the chopping block you've set up next to the line, one hand on the tongs and another on the slicer, and now both eyes are on the petit filet to your right, to that wen of fat on the side that's complementing just so the marbled red flesh. To your left, the porterhouses need to be turned, need to flip down now onto their backsides if there's any hope of keeping the 'alla fiorentina' in the title of the nightly special, chef, and the dance of the olive oil and the lemon wedges and the cracked pepper on the plated Tuscan beans is keeping time in your head, but you're somehow not watching where your right hand is going, and then you don't even know you're bleeding onto the food until you hear the spurt of blood hit the coals below the great hefts of beef.

In the length of that slow synapse, you remember there's always that full breadth of a few seconds between the cut and the pain, that timer of injury between what your skin knows and, milliseconds later, what the brain will. This delay's always fascinated you. It's the act of watching a group of terrified translators arguing about the best way to warn the body of an attack, their message being sent off into the waves as late as they can possibly wait. And now here it is. That sound, that gush of thick red liquid onto the coals as it vaporizes, comes right before the sharpness, and now you're raw and bloodier than the porterhouses.

But there's no time, not with those poor bisteccas on the heat. The T-bones speak up at you as you wince from the knife's edge, a pair of stuttering hunks of meat with an important message you know already in your heart: it's t- t- time, man. It's t- t- time to take us off the grill, chef, and it's t- t- time to let us rest and soak up on the block. It's now or never if you're going to keep their pretty insides rare like the recipe calls for, and you've got the choice here between saving their souls or patching up a slice to the cleft of your left hand. Bisteccas alla fiorentina or Band-Aids, chef. You choose.

But there's no choice here. Instead, there's only you and a flame and a pair of porterhouses that need to go out to that last and very lucky couple in the dining room, the ones who have officially scratched out the nightly entree special with their requests, the ones who are depending on you to get this old-country Spanish dish just so very right and right now, what with the potential for their rave reviews on the restaurant sites and the recommendation pages on the line. Every dish, you realize—now that everyone gets a voice and everyone gets an opinion—is another chance to keep your customers coming back and to keep that line of hungry people firmly stationed out the door. Besides, you ask yourself, who was the cheap bastard who only ordered thirty of these T-bones for the dinner rush? Who, you wonder, would be so concerned with the books and the black ink on the ledger that he wouldn't leave room for error on the entrees, not even when your sweet walrus of a man, Cliff, raised an eyebrow at the low number?

And then, of course, the blood still dripping down your palm, still riveting down your fingertips onto the grooved floor, you remember that it was and always has been you, chef.

T- T- Time's up, and so here come the porterhouses. Your blood, you reckon, will seep up right alongside the juices from the cow back into the beef, if it hasn't been burned into the char already. Your wound, you know, will either get infected with salmonella or E.coli, and there will be topical antibiotics to follow after the dinner rush, but there will also always be the chance at five stars and burning recommendations and the name of your and Cliff's restaurant, Modena, at the top of everyone's favorite kitchens in town.

But when that timer above the grill beeps out the end of the five minutes of rest, the plates still hot with the beans and the lemon and the garnishing greens, there's still the need to check for the unmistakable blush of red in the flesh, whether it's come from you or the livestock, you're not sure, but there's nothing to see here, folks, and so you meet your waiter's eyes at the line, give him the nod, and then watch as he gazelles his way out around the corner and to the hungry couple that's ordered the last pair of specials for the night, the last two of the thirty T-bones, and you hope they don't send that hard choice back to you and your shame in the kitchen, the red of your blood still dripping onto the white plate and the pink porterhouse from where it shouldn't be.

But there it is. There's your set of five yellow, digital stars on *Yowl*, unbelievably and undeniably from that same couple from the evening's dining room.

"Best steaks I've ever had in my life," the subject line says. "I'm not normally a fan of being served just big chunks of meat, but I ate the whole thing! So did my girlfriend!"

The winking smiley face after the last remark makes you grin, but then that's when you remind yourself about the other reviews. There are the four-and-a-half star lines that paid more attention to the bartender's ass than it did the cuisine, or the low lights in the restaurant and the bohemian atmosphere more than the flavor of the food. There are the bits that type out "really good food" but not the explicit "great," the rows and rows of customer opinions that keep Modena popular but not recognized for the skills of those who feed all the hungry people at the door. A man can only offer up himself, you know?

But this guy? The five-star fellow? He can't quit over those porterhouses. Good for him, though, since those thick darlings take a careful eye and a hot set of coals.

"Hey, Cliff!" you yell. Gold chain you bought him last year for the anniversary dangling around his neck, Cliff looks up from behind the bar. You watch his bushy arms and mustache and eyebrows working over a beer and what looks like a simple egg & mayo sandwich on a tapas plate, and you love him again for his pure tastes in life.

"Hmm?" He comes back with a mumble, a whisper. This is a banquet hall of a place, a wood-studded studio of chairs and walnut booths and free-standing walls with metal-jack lanterns that hang overhead and droop down from a vaulted ceiling, a place carved by you both together, and Cliff has yet to learn how to yell.

"Those T-bones from tonight?"

Cliff nods his head as you yell back.

"Next time around, we're ordering fifty instead of thirty!" You make a promise you will do this, will force your co-owner, your partner, your lover, and *Modena's* manager to accept that the number of special-order steaks you want stocked in the cooler is going to jump by a good two-thirds.

Cliff nods his head again like a fishing lure, grumbles something audible to himself and to no one else, and then goes back to the dripping egg on the plate.

In between the soft bump of the last of the waitstaff's restocked salt & pepper mills on the wooden tables and the scrape of Cliff's fork to his teeth, you remember what's bothering you about the evening: the sole and solitary five-star run on the bisteccas. If they were good across the board, you reason, those five-star comments on the steaks alone would be pouring in by now.

You imagine the number of duos and trios and quartets who have gone off into the night, whose dates and evenings have hit a brief lull in conversation and activity, whose hands should have by now dug into their pockets and mined out their phones, which should have by now been graced by the bright whites and reds of *Yowl* and the blues and yellows of *ForksUnderKnives* and all the rest of the review sites. Out of the thirty times where those T-bones were seared and served up to the hungry, only one couple had enjoyed it enough to give Modena their full praise of the flesh, and, aside from the sound of Cliff's gentle chewing from across the parquet floor, that's been the thing that's been gnawing at you just as much as the scabbed over slice in your left hand. Five stars for the blueberry-infused ganache, you read. Five stars for the baked-in-house brioche, and five stars for the copper cups for the Moscow Mules at the bar, and five stars for the wasabi remoulade, but no one loves those porterhouses like the last couple of the night did.

The wound still smolders with as much heat as the quieted grill in the kitchen now, warm and tender but dying. It's a smile of red on the webbing of your skin, a crescent moon of a gash that's going to need some antibiotics and a muslin wrap for the night back at your and Cliff's apartment two floors up. Between the tallies and the sips from the gin & tonic now magically in front of you—a tip of the head from Eduardo, your sous, of thanks—you start to rub at the fresh line of the scab and ask yourself, What was the difference, chef?

One of the first things they taught you at Tri-County Culinary was beef. They started you off with food safety, a reminder that the protein should just touch 125°F before you could start playing with it, and then they let you out to dream and experiment in the kitchen. They let you grill and braise and broil the pink chunks of flesh from every point between rare and well done and all the bubblegum-colored places in between. They taught you the cuts of the cow, from the chuck to the shanks and the sweet delights of the loins. They showed you the importance of letting the great hunks rest after their wearying battles with heat, so that the juices and water from the flesh could pool back into their centers before another knife was allowed in them, and they tested you on these things.

Once the chefs at the school knew you could work your way around flesh, they knew they could trust you with the secrets of how to grind your own pasta and how to ferment your own cheese, how to poach an egg and how to whip your own mayonnaise. They taught you to respect what you took from the farmer and the butcher. They taught you to turn pigments into paintings, and so you believed the two years spent in aprons was worth it.

Three months into the program, you and the fourteen other students in your cohort were told to meet near the stoves in the test kitchen. You were each given a small tenderloin, and you were told to get it to a medium-rare state, by whatever means you held in your heart. In the middle of the great stainless-steel island in the center of the kitchen, there stood a glass beaker of a dark liquid, unlabeled and only a liter's worth of whatever it was. There was acid in the air that singed the hairs in your nose, and it burned sweetly.

So you fired up the grill and waited. While a dozen of your peers grabbed sauté pans from the overhead hooks and flipped switches for the gas burners, you and a corn-fed brute from Nebraska lit the gas to the grills in the back of the kitchen and waited the five minutes it took to heat patiently, arms crossed and silent, looking all the while at either the pans on the fires around you or the sweat on the students' foreheads.

One of the younger kids from New York had pulled out the hot water bath and set the *sous vide* cooker to 145°F. Once he dropped the bagged steak into the heated pool, he stood back and crossed his arms like you and Nebraska did, poking at the clear plastic every so often to make certain it was still warm.

You remember the rest of the kitchen grew irritated with you and Nebraska for the extra time it would take to grill the beef at a low temp. There was the matter of the rich liquid in the center of the kitchen, they seemed to import, and there was sleep to get and knives to clean before it. But you turned your back to them and gently pounded the flesh with a tenderizer as the grill continued to warm, so that its iron grate would be barely hot enough to receive the tender slabs and sear them to a light and crusty char. When the both of you flipped the loin, you noticed how one of the instructors grabbed a large sauce pot and set it atop one of the gas ranges with a vacuum hood, and how the fan was turned on right after the dark liquid from the center steel-top was added to the pot to heat.

The kitchen smelled immediately of vinegar, you remember, of balsamic grape must and mash where the applied heat was working its way onto the hexane rings of the aromatics and sending them flying into the nostrils of the chefs standing next to the lines. Its sharp notes filled your chests and forced some of you to cough from the acrid scent, and this was when the instructor tapped the vacuum hood and reminded you of the importance of knowing what to cook was akin to knowing where to cook properly. But the voice that followed while the vinegar roiled on the stove said only, "Please slice your beef and arrange the pieces out on a plate once they've had the chance to rest."

And so your cohort did, right before your own tenderloin had the chance to come to rest. Behind you, the sound of a dozen or so chefs' knives chimed together like a chorus of drawn swords, armaments at the ready, and there was only the matter of timing on your part to take place in the song. Around you, the air was caustic and pert, and you wondered what the instructor had in store.

At the stove, the head chef was busy swirling the final mix of what the balsamic vinegar had reduced into now, and it was your turn to slice through the grain of the filet. This took a long time, you remember, because you wanted your slices to be thin and delicate, like a carpaccio, but the cooked beef wasn't so easy to navigate as what a rarer slab would have yielded up. And that was okay. Even this early in the morning, the beef would be welcome as a breakfast, as a highlight in a brunch meal, as an early dinner.

Fifteen plates sat on the edge of the center counter, with fifteen different choices of how the tenderloins were cut. You were happy that each of your peers' steaks had that warm pink center in each of their cuts, and that each of them had developed a light browning on the outside of the flesh from the heat and the Maillard reactions that each of you had studied from the expensive textbooks. This was a good thing, and so were the choices of how the steaks had been sliced: from thin, like yours, to cubes and strips and, in the case of Nebraska's loin, thick tips of beef the width of a deck of playing cards.

In the center, the instructor swirled a thick syrup of the balsamic vinegar he'd boiled down on the stove beforehand. The steel ladle sloshed its way around the metal tureen, and the air was still pungent with the evaporated fumes.

"Take a bite first," the man said, still swirling.

And you did. You watched Nebraska's washed fingers pull up one of the great beef tips and stuff it into the space between his incisors. A younger, tattooed student down the line made a face at one of the cubes she had cooked but put it in her mouth anyway, and you watched as the enjoyment and curiosity from whatever was there before started to edge away. For you, though, the thin slice on your plate was a welcome treat, a good finish to the eggs you'd made that morning on the apartment stove, with Cliff standing next to you and slavering in his underwear. The beef was still warm near the edges, but you could taste how the kosher salt had made it down into the meat's cool center. This, you knew and would forever know, was a pleasure.

Without a word, the instructor moved from plate to plate, ladling out a small tablespoon of the syrup onto each row of the remaining cuts. He painted with the ladle, pouring it evenly and across each of the sections like the small cup was a brush of dark pastels, and he barely had enough for the last plate, yours, but he smiled at you as though it would be enough.

"This is an old magic trick in the kitchen," he said. "A substitution of one thing for another." There was a beat in there, like he was letting his words cool to completion. "Dig in."

And you did. Whatever the balsamic vinegar had reduced to, it was a good and flavorful thing. It was sweet, with notes of cherry and caramel and deep red wines in there, and it brought out the chords of the steak in a way you hadn't known before, the way only an acidic flavor like this could. To your left, Nebraska gnawed on the second of the three hunks he'd cut his sirloin into, closing his eyes in there for a moment and letting the flavors collide. You did the same.

"Good, right?" the instructor said. "Good balsamic vinegar flavor in there?"

You nodded.

"Here's the thing, though," he said. "Those bottles you buy in the stores? Those great jugs in the school pantries? That's not real balsamic vinegar."

You remember the looks of all those faces in the kitchen.

"Not the real deal. Real balsamic has its own set of rules and preparations, and it's regulated in Italy like wine's regulated in France." You remember the instructor's words settled then, like the caramel flavor of the reduction in your mouth. "This stuff, though? Industrial-grade imitation stuff, like off-the-shelf vanilla is to real vanilla extract. Same basic flavor patterns to the untrained, but noticeable enough if you measure and taste it." He pulled out a salad oil bottle from the length of table behind his back, then swirled the dark fluid in the glass around before pushing away the remnants from the steel tureen on the countertop. "But this batch, dear students, is pure. Balsamic vinegar of the Modena region. It's the condiment version of the real, $200-a-bottle stuff, which should never touch heat in the first place."

Suddenly, you remember, the flavor in your mouth started to pale, to go off in a way you didn't enjoy. You remember how Nebraska looked at the great, last hunk of flesh on his plate and turned his eyes back to you in disappointment.

"When you cook for hungry people, you must give them your best, each and every time," the instructor said, the smell of vinegar still lingering around him. "You must give them your full talents."

In the kitchen that morning, the only things you and your cohort could hear, then, were the sound of the fan overhang, the clapping of a pair of tongs somewhere off down the hallway, and the head chef's words like mallets on a kettle drum.

"Above all," he hummed, "you must give of yourself."

Come Friday night, it's you and Eduardo, the sous, and even Cliff back there on the line, with Eduardo busting ass on plating and sautéing the Swiss chard & portobello confits that match nicely with the petit filets, thank you very much, and with Cliff checking and double-checking orders as they pile up on the server's station, his white eyebrows and sea lion mustache bobbing as he nods against the instructions between rare, medium-well, and everything in between, and there's not a single soul in the house tonight who would dare order something so beautiful to be done up overly *well* and beyond recognition, not tonight, but there you are above the cast-iron pans and the gas, wondering why in the hell you offered pan-seared filets when the grill heat would have been sufficient, thank you also very much, but what are you going to do on this night of graduation at the local prep school academy, with all the parents and grandparents and boosters and wealthy alumni, all of them hungry and waiting for the weekend special?

From the ranges, you can hear the din of the dining room, the clinking of glasses and plates against the wooden tabletops and the soft house music riding the undercurrent of *Modena's* interior. This was a touch you didn't think Cliff had in him—the ability to listen past the desire for old-time country, as he enjoys, through to the need for something inaudible past a beat below the level of conversation—and you appreciate your partner in this all the more for it. For a Friday night, there's more of the high pitch of children's voices in the air, more family and friends' kids, you imagine, given the occasion, but your fears of having the place turn into a glorified family restaurant are gone once the orders for the filets keep washing in through the window. Grade schoolers, you know damn well, chef, aren't ordering tenderloins.

Just after happy hour, it's slow going: a couple of special orders here and there, a trio at times, and there's nothing to do but look bored and drink water with Eduardo next to you while the white-square ceramic plates keep waiting to receive whatever's been ordered. The range stays hot, the cast-iron pans keep getting used and then sent back to be scraped and seasoned and returned, and the night drives through. Above and around you, your variation on a thick Tom Yum soup wafts through the kitchen and the dining room, and the soup is more popular than the beef.

But now here's the stampede of orders you've been waiting for: the eight-top and the ten-top, both of them together, a rip of dishes that will either go to Eduardo for delivery to the kitchen crew for the usual run of the menu, or to you for the specials. There's the mark of the Alfredo mac & cheese dishes—four kids at the table, no doubt—and a haricot vert salad, and a Spanish-style burger that'll sit above a bed of beets and citrus in the brioche below it, and one for the grilled tofu that someone else will have to take care of in the kitchen. But then, of course, come the orders for the filets, eight of them total between the ten- and the eight-top, and it's all at once, and there's only the hope that the steaks will match each other in terms of heat and thickness and marbling and time.

You watch as pat after pat of salted butter gets thrown into the pans, each of them heating and melting into a run of the oil underneath and the rich scum on the top of the pond, and then in go the filets, four to a pan, two great cast-iron beasts sitting in front of you on the stoves, with their too-hot-to-touch handles and their measured, even heat blasting off from the rims, but then it's time for what you hope will move you from good to great in a single night.

"Eduardo, man," you say, and Eduardo comes.

"Chef?" he asks. He'll run this restaurant someday, you know, long after you and Cliff are down in Belize plating rock shrimp ceviche out of cabanas, unless Eduardo finds the money to set up his own bistro in another city. Good for him either way, you think. Good for him.

"Out on the floor," you whisper under the din, "there's some poor customer who's ordered a tofu cake in the middle of a bunch of omnivores, so if you could grill it and give it a delicate touch, I'd owe you a beer after the shift tonight."

Eduardo stares at you and nods with all the seriousness of a coronary, says, "Yes, chef," and moves over to the walk-in to find the tub of water with the tofu cakes inside, passing Cliff and Cliff's broom mustache along the way, who looks like he's deep in thought about where he might find another set of black ramekins.

"We making some money, baby?" you ask him.

Cliff coughs, still uncomfortable calling you pet names in public or, for the kitchen, in semi-public. "We're making some money," he says, and you swear you can see a grin at the corners of his lips. You watch him disappear into the bakery stacks.

And this, chef, is when you dash over to the sink to wash your hands one last time before this all goes raw, and you hope you're not making what will be the worst culinary decision in your life, but there's always next week, you know, and that's when the soap and the hot water hit your fingers. This is purification, you realize, but it'll also probably help with the ritual of flavor.

Eduardo and Cliff gone, the line empty save for you and your left hand, chef, you take the knife at your side and let it cut through the skin of your hand, right there at the familiar webbing, and it hurts so bad, but so do most things in this world, and you're busy thinking back to Tri-County Culinary's tureen of balsamic vinegar and Nebraska and the taste of tenderloin in your mouth, to the familiar ladling of the thick syrup onto the hot chunks of beef, which is what you're doing now, chef, a deep red now instead of the familiar black, and you're hoping there will be the same pleasure as the couple that came in the week before, and that there will be the gustatory nod from person to person at each table, a signal that this meal is not just good but great.

But I Can Only Do it Once

Before the fire blows out a corner of the house where Jack Marsh and his family live, before my father's oxygen tank overheats and sends shrapnel into the neighbor's yard, he opens his eyes in the rental Trendelenburg bed, licks his lips, and tells me a story.

"So there's this talent scout."

My father's face is now as gaunt and sagging as his scrotum, which my mother and I are in charge of wiping these days. He is blotchy and bruised in improbable places, like the top of his head, where all his hair has fallen out but is beginning to grow back in. We've been told this is what happens when you stop chemotherapy. He will do this occasionally: wake up from the middle of a horrible sleep, pick up on a conversation he thinks he's having or one we've had already and from much earlier in the day. We talk a lot about breakfast.

"And he's taking appointments for new acts, and all these people are coming through the door, lining up and waiting for their minute with him."

My father licks at the corner of his mouth. His breath smells like oatmeal, and although it's late for tonight, a Wednesday, I've been having difficulty sleeping. Sleep feels less and less necessary, but I'm busy reading my Civics primer and learning about U.S. senatorial protocol. Concerned about the dark patches I'm wearing below my eyes most days, my mother has yelled up that it's time for bed soon, but my father either doesn't hear her or doesn't care.

"Dad," I say. "Hey, are you thirsty?"

He picks at the new Fentanyl patch that's driving concentrated morphine into his skin.

"And the talent scout hasn't seen anything new all day." He pauses, looks down at his arm. "So he's just about to close up shop when this clown comes in and starts juggling."

Next to his bed is the plastic water pitcher he's brought home from his last trip to the hospital. I shake it. Ice clicks at the sides as the water sloshes.

"And the talent scout says he's not interested. Starts packing up his briefcase and papers."

I fill his cup up again and reposition the straw. Before coming home on hospice care, my father would receive straws in his drinks at restaurants without asking for them, pull them out, and lay them by the side of the glass. He would gulp and leave grease on the rims as he would drink.

"So the clown jumps on a unicycle and starts pedaling around the office carpet. The talent scout? He's not even looking up."

My father, Jack Marsh, blinks on and off and on again. He stares at me like he's sleeping, and I have to stare back to see if he's unconscious most days now.

"So now the clown knows he's in trouble. And he's desperate. So he says all quiet-like, 'Hold your horses; you've got to see this.' From some pocket or something, okay, he whips out a bottle of nitroglycerin. Drinks that down like it's lemonade." He slurs out 'lemonade' and rolls his eyes. "Then he pulls out a stick of dynamite and munches it down to the wick like a carrot."

I'm trying to remember that the Vice President has the power to break a tie in the U.S. Senate. I will be quizzed on the material in the morning.

"Then from nowhere—this guy's a magician, too, apparently—he shows off this red can of gasoline, slurps it down from the spigot and wipes his mouth clean. Now this? This is where it gets interesting."

My father stares at me, at my book.

"They still have talent scouts, right?"

He slips his head down and closes his eyes again. I wait for five minutes before I push the cup of water with the straw a little closer to his lips.

My mother and I have always had the benefit of knowing exactly what to get my father for Christmas or for his birthday. If it might manage to make him a little safer at night when he gets called out of the station on a run, he'll cherish the gift and he'll donate the old equipment to whomever shows the most interest in it. The twelve-cup coffee maker is donated to my mother's office once he receives the four-cup pot that can brew in five minutes. The standard bolt cutters are given to one of the lieutenants a few weeks after he opens up the new pair, the ones with the rubberized grips and the Teflon-coated pincers. And I take with me to Table Rock Lake one year the old MagLite he handed to me once I buy him a special-edition halogen that burns through fog, batteries, and his patience. Using the old flashlight as a beacon, I light up the dark water near the rocky beach and watch two teenagers make out for a brief moment with their shirts off.

"Kill the lights, perv!" the girl shouts out to me.

This is my first association of breasts with death threats.

An act that started in kindergarten, my father will trade off with the assigned safety officer to run the equipment inspections every three months in the corridors of Timmons Elementary or Dwight D. Eisenhower Middle School, and he'll always volunteer to bring by one of the trucks on the annual Fire Safety Day. My friends will ask for stories from when he has the occasional night at the station, and I'll leave out his complaints of paperwork and budget cuts and fill them in with standby favorites of his calls out to Fourth of July parties gone awry or kitchen fires sprung out of tipped oil bottles.

To impress girls, I tell them about the time he found a head wrapped up in a fence of barbed wire near a car accident, a story I've heard every so often when my father is on the phone to old friends, or when he's busy working down a six-pack and I'm up late with homework.

One of my strongest memories of him comes from a blend of times we've gone to the mall, of instances when he'll remark about the proximity of a half-dressed mannequin display to a fire exit or point out where a fake plant will be in the way of an accessible alarm. While he should just make a note of it and report it to the responsible comm officer to deal with out on the next inspection, I remember despairing over the moments when he'll approach the poor man at the cash register or, worse, the large-breasted sister of one of my friends who recognizes me from school as she is folding sweaters.

My mother tolerates this and other embarrassing moments better than I do. When she was younger, she tells me, she'd married a smart fireman, one who wasn't interested as much in the heroics as he was in making people safe. He cooks, he cleans, and he exercises enough on the training and recertification course to come home with muscle, which my mother seems to appreciate. My cousins, Greg and Vic, twin boys who stay with us when their parents are fighting and who gossip like the cheerleaders they try to talk up at the bus stop, tell me they once heard from their mother that my father was 'hung,' and that she's jealous of who her sister has married, and that's why she and the twins' father fight so much.

"So that's it, then," Vic says. "Your dad's got a huge cock."

"Massive," Greg says.

We spend the next thirty minutes in my bedroom, measuring our flaccid penises in comparison to nearby objects. As a thirteen-year-old, I can safely say I am just as thick as a cherry-scented magic marker but not nearly as long. Greg, however, who is fourteen and has long fingers, is half an inch longer than Vic, who feels uncomfortable about the fact that his penis is more bulbous two-thirds the way up than it is at the base. He feels better, he tells us, after finding one of my mother's antique letter openers and seeing that he's about the same shape as its handle. I'd like to think that he's decent enough at the time to wipe off the opener before returning it to my mother's bureau.

During the 1992 Summer Olympics, when the twins are staying with us again—"Their parents are going on vacation, kiddo," my mother reminds me, "down to Cozumel"—my cousins tell me of their plan to capture my father's penis in full profile.

"I'm probably going to get married someday," Vic tells me. "A guy's got to know how big he needs to be to keep his wife happy, right?"

We are eating oatmeal at the time that I'm not able to finish.

"Shape and girth, man," Greg says. "You've got to know about these things."

"So we don't get enough life lessons camping?" I ask. "See, you two know how to cook eggs over a fire. You know bow lines. You know how to change a tire on a switchback."

"Yeah, Uncle Jack's advice on bringing enough clean socks is really helpful," Vic says. "You know what would be good, though? Tips on how to make a girl moan. There's not just high school to think of, dick. There's college."

I try to explain to Vic and Greg that what makes my mother happy is when my father poaches salmon or keeps his risotto creamy, or when he hires a babysitter for me so they can go to a restaurant or a movie alone, but the twins sound determined. At nights, when we're supposed to be watching women's volleyball matches or pole vaults, broadcast from a high-res feed from Barcelona, my cousins make it a mission to stumble into my father whenever he's trying to take a piss or when he's in the middle of a shower.

"Sorry, Uncle Jack," Vic'll say quickly, barely covering his attempt to stare at my father's crotch.

"We didn't mean to," Greg will say.

"Boys, goddamn it, this is getting out of hand." My father never rages, just furrows, and he'll smile after swearing most times. He chalks it up to teenage stupidity, something he hasn't quite seen in me yet.

"Yet," he tells me on occasion.

When it finally does happen, Greg and Vic open up the door to the bathroom and catch my father wiping his ass with one leg on the rim of the tub.

Over cannelloni and spinach that night, I hear, "Victor! Gregory! God damn it," followed quickly by the almost unheard-of sound in the fire captain's house: an interior door being locked.

On the evening we're supposed to watch Jennifer Capriati win the women's singles in tennis, ready and sweating in the tight spaghetti-strapped top and skirt, we're instead driven by my father to the only open bookstore that night, marched down to the Psychology and Sexuality aisle, and forced to purchase *The Bright Lad's Guide to Sex* with our combined pool-cleaning money. On the ride back to the house, while my cousins properly learn how to unroll and put on a condom, I'm treated to a lecture I've only heard twice before but one that I've mostly memorized by now.

"Do you know why we don't lock doors in the house, boys?" my father asks evenly from the front seat.

"Yes, sir," I say.

"Nope," Vic says. I watch his fingertips run over a pencil sketch of a woman's spread vulva.

"No, sir," Greg says, stifling laughter.

"You want to enlighten your cousins, Andy?"

"Yes, sir," I cough. Vic is bent over the book now, dissecting pictures with captions explaining how it's perfectly okay for erect penises to be straight or curved. "In case of emergency, a locked door on the inside of a house can present an unnecessary risk to occupants and to first-responders at the scene. Incapacitated occupants can become trapped or further endangered behind locked doors, either through unexpected paralysis or loss of consciousness from smoke inhalation, concussion, um—."

"Exposure to harmful chemicals," my father interjects. "Greg! Are you getting this?"

Greg's eyes are locked onto a description of an aureole. "Yep."

"And exposure to harmful chemicals," I finish. "The longer an individual remains in a burning building, the likelier the chance of fatality. Locked interior doors heighten this chance unnecessarily."

At home, we are denied the replays and highlight reels of Capriati's win, and we are sent to bed with the book to read.

Vic asks me that night, huddled under his covers with a borrowed MagLite, "Ever seen a picture of the clitoral hood?"

Just a few years before the explosion, on the night when the Dream Team beats Croatia to win the gold, during a period when the twins and I have expressed interest in not being bothered while we watch Jordan, Bird, and Johnson dunk over the hopes of Eastern Europe and the rest of the modern world, and when my parents have looked at each other, smiled, looked back at us and said they'll probably just go to bed early, then, Vic, Greg, and I make the mistake of catching my parents fucking in the yellow lamplight of their bedroom.

To call it a 'mistake,' though, doesn't take into account Vic's cropped ear to their door, or the wild encouragement Greg gives me to come over and listen right alongside him while Chuck Daly reminisces on the post-game interview. We've come up from the living room into the kitchen in search of a two-liter of soda, and then there's Vic and Greg, padding up the stairs and being careful to avoid the spots of creaking floorboard.

"What the hell are you doing?" I whisper, as loudly as I can manage.

"Jesus Christ, we're taking notes, you little bitch," Greg spits down at me as I start to follow.

"Seriously, that thing's huge," Vic hisses. "How have you not seen it?"

I have before, on accident. It's a part of my father's body, like his right forearm, the one with the old burn marks he tries to cover up when he's away from the house with long sleeves.

As Barkley scores the 103rd point that night, I hear my mother gasp out and whisper to my father, "Goddamn, that's good. Roll over and hand me the bottle."

It's one of the first times I ever heard my mother swear—possibly the first for my cousins, who are now stifling the giggles—and then there's the rush of me yelling out 'No!' while Greg opens the door and angles over to the left next to Vic for a better view while my mother grabs the sheets from below her frame.

Later that night, my father calls my aunt and uncle and tells them about the event, and the twins are put on the phone, one after the other, and they cry and apologize after being told that their behavior is making their parents very frustrated, and that this crap is making it difficult to enjoy the very much needed break that my aunt and uncle require, and that, yes, their mother and father are on the verge of separation if they don't return to that previous and wonderful level of intimacy they're both craving. For a little over an hour afterward, my mother explains sex to her ten-year old and his eleven-year-old cousins, in the middle of which my father asks, "Don't you kids have friends with porn?"

"No," Greg says, squirming, "but we do have a question."

Vic, who looks squeamish after listening to my mother, turns to my father and asks, "Uncle Jack, does it stay that big all the time?"

"No, Victor. Not all the time."

The twins are right, though. Glistening with lube in the bedroom light, my father had looked happy in that moment just before realizing his son and nephews were in the room, that there were boys around him who were curious and horny and without friends who stole their fathers' copies of *Penthouse* to share.

Sixteen and sullen now, the twins have come to pick me up for a movie in the mustard-yellow Oldsmobile my aunt has given them moments before my father calls the house to find out what his group number is on his insurance plan. Later, he tells us that he has twice seen a reddish tinge in his urine at work, which is why he's gone to visit his primary, who tells him to roll up his sleeve so a tattooed man in the clinic lab can pull seven tubes of blood after my father pees into a cup. We wait for two days before his follow-up, which my father insists on going to alone. When he comes back, he brings in a blue folder with him that contains printouts and patient-information forms, and he announces it.

"Well, fuck." The blue folder has a white label on it with his name, date of birth, and an account number. I wonder if the doctors know about his penicillin allergy. "You know what? That attic's getting cleaned anyway."

This is probably the typical reaction of a family who receives similar news. My mother sits with my father on the couch and cries and asks questions about his pancreas, and my father says things but always includes the mention of the appointment with the radiation therapist on Monday.

The appointment with the therapist on Monday involves a CT scan, an MRI, more blood work, and a follow-up for a session where a team of radiation therapists essentially try to burn a hole around a dark spot on my father's pancreas. Later, he goes to an oncologist for two rounds of chemotherapy treatments, which last for seven months, and then he checks into the hospital for a few days as a lieutenant at the county offices is promoted to Assistant Fire Chief. In the last few weeks of his life, Jack Marsh is visited by hospice nurses who make kind faces at my mother while I wash dishes and change light bulbs around the house.

And then there's the explosion. Jack has promised us it won't be the cancer that will kill him, and we smirk in front of him because we're uncomfortable around death, and because my father says this with a grin on his face, as well.

On the evening after the funeral, the twins pick me up again and drive to my uncle's house, which is filled with boxes of pornography, and is dark and empty for a few days while my cousins' father is out of town, and they take off their shoes and muffle the occasional sob as one and then both of them hand me shots of blue alcohol that burn as they slide down the throat.

When my mother and my aunt call the house, frantic and looking for their sons, she sounds together relieved and terrified. When we hang up the phone, I tell Vic and Greg that our mothers are coming to get us. Greg pours us another shot of blue liquor, and we toss the shot glasses back, slamming them on the kitchen counter once we finish.

"Do you remember the last trip to Table Rock?" I ask.

"Was that the one where we saw the skinny kids fucking?" Vic sniffs at his glass. "Because that was awesome. I should have brought my camera."

"The one after," I say. "The board games? The raccoon?"

"Oh, yeah," Greg says. "Your dad gave those people shit about the bonfire, right?"

I nod and stop talking. I look around at my uncle's house. It's part of an affordable subdivision he moved into after the divorce.

"Was that it?" Vic asks.

"That's it," I say.

On the last drink, Greg picks up his glass, fingers out a drop of blue from the bottom as he pulls a piece of shrapnel from a ruptured oxygen tank, and says into the air, "To Uncle Jack, the well-hung man."

Chemotherapy makes sense to my father as long as he thinks about it like it's a homework assignment. It's planned, it's draining, but it's on the syllabus, and he feels bad about having his friends in the department cover for him over those long mornings or afternoons he's scheduled at the treatment center.

My mother buys him Louis Lamour paperbacks from weekend garage sales, and I lend him the books we're reading in our English classes after I use them for reports and essays. He rips through them in the plastic-draped recliners in the clinic's treatment area, or he dozes off and wakes up to find his saline bags empty next to the spent doses of compounds that are trying to kill off his pancreas slowly and efficiently.

Between the stopovers the nurses make at my father's chair to attach and detach a pulse oximeter, he asks about the books some of the oncologists keep on a glass-paneled shelf behind the counters. These are the prize donations made to an oncology clinic in western Missouri: a leather-bound Bible, an older edition of Taber's Medical Cyclopedia, an ancient textbook on hematology, and a book about the history of cancer and chemotherapy. While the nurses won't let my father take home the history book, they bring it to him on the days when he's getting dosed and doesn't have reading material with him from home.

These are the stories Jack Marsh tells me as I stay up and work on class assignments or try to read patient information labels on the bags and boxes he receives from the clinic and pharmacy. They don't involve the speed of a fire truck as it barrels down a residential area or emergency axes being used on door frames, or times when the force of water flying out of a hose knocks a rookie on his feet; instead, I get history lessons on medicine he's learned during the day, filtered and summarized as he drifts to sleep on the couch or in the wooden chair at my desk.

"You have friends who smoke, Andy?"

"One kid. Three, maybe." I run through the roster. "Like five? There's one guy in marching band who's about to get expelled, I think."

"Pot?"

"Some of the same." A ninth-grade girl I know with blonde hair, long scarves, and breasts is a dealer, and I'm giving serious consideration to making pot part of my daily regimen. She smells like hard work, like a hair salon at the end of the day. I lie to my father. "I don't, though. Smells bad."

Jack blinks his eyes and rubs them. "Well, that's okay, kiddo. Pot's not that bad. But don't tell Mom I said that." He opens them up again. "They're trying to approve some cannabis—the stuff in marijuana that makes you hungry, okay?—to get chemo patients to eat."

My father is skinnier at this point. His hands and feet are rough, peeling, and red. His lips are always chapped.

"Would that help you?" I ask.

He has to think about this. "It might," he says. "Might slow things down a bit."

When he was first told about the chemo regimen he would go through, my father did what a lot of other patients did and shaved his head in advance. When it would try to grow back in patches, he'd whittle it down with his razor and try not to cut himself.

"Some of the drugs I'm on thin out the blood," he'd explain.

This is before we learn about the metastases, about the hidden neoplastic cells that fire off somewhere else into his system. We learn that the tumors have spread to his liver after his abdomen begins to swell on the side, and after he groans when his oncologist palpates the bulge. We take him in for a CT and an MRI when he starts to complain of dizziness and constant headaches, and that's when he finds out that the malignant cells have slipped through his bloodstream and up into his brain.

A few nights after he learns the results of the scans, he tells us to move him from the bedroom into the guest room, onto the bed my parents had bought for my grandmother a few years ago. On the side of the rig is a control pad that lifts the mattress up at the head or the back or the legs, and my mother, aunt, and I hoist Jack Marsh onto the bed frame that doesn't whine with weight as we lay him in, and then almost immediately we hear the spin of the servos as my father positions himself upright so the coughing will almost stop.

"Now this isn't so bad," he says, and my mother begins to cry. My father has told her that he doesn't want to wake her in the night each time he has to get up or shift in his sleep. After she excuses herself, Jack whispers to me, "I am going to miss watching the nurses' asses, though."

"If doctors get to work with women like that, you're going to have to pay for medical school," I say. And Jack chuckles, nods, and closes his eyes for a few minutes.

While my father dozes on his narcotics, I stay up and finish my Geometry homework, filling in gaps where I'm given the length of one side of a right triangle and its accompanying angle, and where I'm asked to find the length of the adjacent side. At a little after midnight, I stop penciling in numbers and lay my head on my desk and listen to the quiet in the house. Downstairs, the grandmother clock ticks on the mantle, and there's the noise of cars out on the interstate near the house, and then there is the sound of Jack Marsh just two doors down from me: coughs from a barely lit room; groans from when he changes position in bed; the whine of the gears from the mechanized bed frame each time my father wakes up to change the angle of his head and feet.

On our last trip to Table Rock Lake, two couples were drinking and blasting out pop country music into the nighttime. They'd built a bonfire the park regulations didn't allow, but my father was more concerned about the blaze's proximity to the campers' propane tanks. He didn't know I had followed him over to their campsite, but I watched as he first negotiated with the foursome, asking them to kill the bonfire in exchange for not reporting a noise complaint to the rangers' station. The two women in the group had dark hair that shined in the firelight and faces that reminded me of the co-eds I'd watched on Channel 74, the cable station with the scrambled porn.

When they balked, I watched as one of the men encouraged

his friend to pummel Jack Marsh until he left them alone, yelling at him until the friend agreed and stumbled his way over to my father. I kept quiet as my father backed away from a sloppy left hook and a swing from the right, smiling at him as he pulled the man forward and onto the gravel by his shirt lapels. As the man fumbled his way onto his knees, I watched Jack tip over a metal bucket of beers and ice, using it to scoop up a mound of dirt that he threw onto the fire. Twice more he did this, until my eyes were having trouble adjusting to the new dark, and I heard him come up in front of me before I could see him in the nighttime.

"Don't be like them," he told me, dragging me up by the collar and helping me back to our campsite.

Tonight, homework finished, I creep up to his door in the guestroom and listen to my father, the man who lays on his back in the nighttime and who chants slowly through clenched teeth and sobs into the hiss of a baby monitor, "I'm fucked. I'm fucked. I'm fucked."

A few mornings after hearing my father's strained verses, I bring him up the flavorless cream of wheat he now swallows and share a bowl with him.

"You know how all this started?" he asks. "The chemo?"

I look down and smell the whiffs of brown sugar and raisins from my own bowl.

"Started in '42, okay?" he says, coughing on occasion. "You know the Allies and the Axis Powers? World War II?"

I nod. "Germany and Japan versus the rest of us, right?"

He glares at me. "And Italy, and Hungary, and Romania, and Bulgaria," he said. "Keep reading, history buff. Okay, so the Allies have all these secret mustard gas bombs on a boat sitting off an Italian harbor. Germany blitzes the damn thing, soldiers and civilians go flying into the water, sucking up the mustard gas in there, and then lots of them start dying off. Like hundreds, okay? When these Allied docs show up and perform autopsies, they figure out that a lot of these soldiers' lymph nodes and blood cells had pretty much shut down when they shouldn't have, and they trace this back to the mustard gas bombs."

He waits for me to look up in recognition.

"It was fire, right? Explosions. Bombs going off and all these people in the water with their white and red blood counts all down and droopy, okay?"

"Okay, dad," I say. "I get it."

"Maybe you get it," he says. "Okay, so these doctors think back to World War I, start remembering that they've seen this before, you know? How these suppressed cells happened after exposure to the mustard gas, and that's when they start thinking about mustard gas as a chemotherapy agent. So they send in these docs and researchers and everyone else with a degree on the subject in and tell them to figure out how to turn this into an advantage. And that, kiddo, was the birth of chemotherapy."

He stops to breathe. This is my father imparting a deathbed education on me, which consists primarily of medical trivia and advice on sexual technique.

"That reminds me: you keep condoms with you?"

"I've got two in my backpack," I say. "Vic and Greg bought them. They have the rest."

"Good," Jack says. "By the way, make sure any girl you're with comes first. You be a gentleman and wait your turn."

"What?"

"Trust me: you'll get yours eventually." He rolls his head to the side and stares at me for a moment. "Yeah. Call up your cousins, kiddo. The boys should be listening to this, too."

The old baby monitor that's hooked up in my dad's room comes with a transmitter that broadcasts to two receivers my mother and I carry around. We take turns and trade off with the hospice nurses when they come to the house. They busy themselves with reading or cleaning open surfaces around my father's bed in the guest room.

The rented Trendelenburg most days is propped up at the head, which relieves some of the pressure Jack's torso exerts onto his abdomen. An oxygen tank is clipped into a metal holder at the right corner in the back of the bed. Two more tanks sit against the far wall, one that's full with its blue-plastic safety wrap still affixed and a partially full tank that my father's saved as an additional backup. Each of the hospice nurses have shown and then quizzed my mother and me on the proper handling of the tanks, and my father has nodded and added in a few bits of advice between their questions.

"And that's another reason why you can't let guests smoke in the house," says a burly Croatian in a matching scrub top-and-bottom set that's decorated with puppy dogs, water bowls, and bones. My mother looks on at my father, wincing because her husband is thinner today and because she has never let anyone smoke in the house since we first opened the door.

"No open flames is what she's trying to say," Jack says. His head bobs up and down in a palsy. He's staring at the shelf near the guest room door, where we've stocked his packets of 4x4s, bags of cannulae, and quarts of isopropyl alcohol.

When the hospice tech staff had come to set up my father's room between hospital visits, they installed a motorized lift with a flat canvas pallet to help ease him out of bed. At first, the lift had been stationary, there for him to pull himself up and out of the bed to use the bathroom with our help. Later, we used the rig more frequently. We would pull him up by lowering it down to him directly for the extra help. Later still, when the bedpans became necessary, when his skin sagged and became waxy and sallow, we used the lift to pull up his legs so he could strain and huff out loose stool into the thin plastic pans. He would grunt in pain when the lift was used, and he would tell me to be gentle as I dabbed at his anus with wet, disposable cloths. When he had the ability, he would wheeze, "Never thought you and I would change places, did you?"

"Come on, Dad," I would say. "Not for a couple more decades."

More often, as the bags of saline and dextrose would filter into his bladder, he'd have to urinate into a plastic jar with milliliter marks on the side. If I hadn't seen my father's penis fit into the open and uncapped top, I would have thought it was a clear canteen made by an outdoors company that valued minimalism and compact forms. At the very end, I would help Jack pull down his sweatpants and flop in through the lid. He would stare at a far point in the room, close his eyes, and concentrate, and a thick orange fluid would run down the sides and collect in the bottom.

On the afternoon of the explosion, Jack Marsh looks like he's gotten enough sleep to make it through the day again, and he calls me into the guest room with a request.

"I feel bad," he says. "Never have a moment to yourselves."

My mother has buzzed his hair in the spots where it's coming back in.

"Here's what I want you to do today," he says. "Let me clean up before the nurses get here. Pick up after myself. I feel good."

"Are you hungry?" I ask.

"Not yet," he says. "I feel filthy, though. I'm a fish in a tank."

To prove himself, he pulls over the pulse oximeter. He fits it onto his right index finger and breathes in a few times. It comes up at 83%, the best we've noticed in the last week.

"See?" he says. "This is doing better."

The guest room smells like urine and sweat. Fingerprints smudge the metal rails on his bed.

"You want to clean?"

"Just a little bit. Who's coming in tonight?"

I have to think about this. "Julia," I tell him. "I'm pretty sure."

"God, her and the fucking popcorn." The hospice house schedules Julia for the occasional nighttime session. She cleans, she eats a microwavable entree, she watches DVDs in the eight-hour overnight shift. Her purse is filled with envelopes of ready-to-heat popcorn. "Seriously, the less time she spends up here, the better."

"Okay, dad," I say. "I'll get a rag."

"Yeah, get a rag. A rag and, if we've still got a couple in the box, some of those steel wool scrubbers."

I turn to go down the stairs.

"Hey," he coughs at me.

"What's up?"

"Ammonia," he tells me. "Look for ammonia."

When I come back upstairs, Jack Marsh is looking out the window. My mother is at work but is due home soon, and Julia won't be in until much later.

"I couldn't find the ammonia," I say.

"But there's the steel wool. Good." Jack breathes out, sticks out his hand. "We're going to need ammonia, though. Smells like shit in here." He laughs as I undo the top to a bottle of rubbing alcohol. "Can you run down to the gas station?"

On most days, the alarm on my father's saline pump doesn't go off. When he's on drips of painkillers, we don't hear the beeps we've been warned about because the machine has never backed up or choked the line, not once. We wait for emergencies to happen that never do.

"I won't tell your mother," he says. Pauses. "And get some Carmex, maybe? I'm chapped to hell."

It's eight minutes to the gas station and back. My father's eyebrows arch up, and I think about the first few days of his chemotherapy sessions, to when the nurses would let him rest in the recliners for an hour at a time as he slept.

Jack breathes in and tells me, "Smells like shit in here, doesn't it?"

I recognize some of my father's coworkers at the funeral. I've seen them asleep or playing cards at the stations around town, wherever Jack would pull an emergency shift on occasion. They hug my mother, give her their condolences, and try to rub my shoulders. Some stick out their hands like I'm being welcomed at church.

We have the reception in a side room at the funeral home. Our house has been cordoned off and is now wrapped in clear plastic as the County Housing Authority completes their walkthrough of the explosion and the remnant fire.

Vic and Greg pick me up in their car, and we drive out to my uncle's house, which is where he's come to live after my aunt left him. On the ride there, I play out the new Fire Inspector's conversation with my mother, the one where he tells her that the fire was accidental, that it could have happened just as quickly if I had been in the kitchen downstairs than if I was on my way back from the gas station. That my father died in his sleep from smoke inhalation and not from the blast, that the hospice program's insurance will share the damages with our homeowner's policy.

On the way out to my uncle's house in Olathe, across the state line and past the new strip malls that are decorated with tile and adobe facades, with fountains at the front of their parking lots, the twins and I pass a bricked-up boxing gym with graffiti on the side.

Tabby Jones vs. Headstrong Ed, we read. *Manson Munson vs. The Old Childe. Friday night!*

There's a mural of a buzz-cut man with muscles and veins posing from the chest up, all of it angles and nothing with curves. And then there's a smaller scene on the bricks, with Elmer Fudd and Daffy Duck from the old Warner Brothers cartoons, forearms arched and the both of them staring each other down.

"That reminds me of a joke," I say.

"Whatever you need to get off your chest, dude," says Greg. We turn onto a side road.

"So there's this talent scout."

"What's a talent scout?" Vic asks.

"And he's taking appointments for new acts, and all these people are coming through the door, lining up and waiting to see him."

"Okay."

"And the talent scout hasn't seen anything new all day. He's just about to close up shop when this clown comes in and starts juggling."

"Is this a cartoon?" Vic asks. "Did we watch this recently?"

We pick up speed and start running parallel to the interstate.

"But the talent scout says he's not interested, and he packs up his briefcase and papers. So the clown gets desperate, and he jumps on a unicycle and starts pedaling around the office carpet, but the scout doesn't even bother looking up."

"This is called 'catharsis,' right? Catharsis?" Greg zooms us past cows in pastures and hay bales.

"So now the guy—the clown, okay—he knows he's in trouble. So he stops the scout from getting up and says, "You've got to see this.' And he whips out a bottle of nitroglycerin from one of his pockets and somehow drinks it down like it's water. Next, he pulls out a stick of dynamite and munches on it like it's a carrot. And he's smiling and sweating, and now the talent scout starts paying attention."

"Okay."

"Then from nowhere the clown pulls out of thin air a red can of gasoline, and he pours it over himself and flicks out a match from his pocket."

Greg starts to tap at the steering wheel. "And then he sets himself on fire. Okay, yeah, I've seen the cartoon. Didn't we see that, like, two years ago? A Saturday morning or something?"

"You guessed it. And then he sets himself on fire and disappears in a black flash of smoke. And the talent scout's eyes nearly bug out of his head, and he drops his cigar onto his desk as his jaw just drops."

My cousins, Victor and Gregory, are seventeen and driving against their mother and father's request that they not take the car out without an adult unless it's an emergency. We accelerate and swerve over the top of small hills, and we catch glimpses of dark patches of prairies out west, past Olathe and this side of Kansas. Several of the patches are dark black and singed; they're recovering quickly from the paring and burning season of early spring, and they're working their way back up into the green.

"But then, to the talent scout's surprise, the clown's ashen ghost turns the knob to the scout's office door and walks back in to the thunderous applause of the talent scout. And the talent scout is excited and yelling, 'That was amazing! That was fantastic! The crowds are going to love it'!"

Each season, after the winds and the ground would begin to warm up, my father and the rest of the fire crews in the county would start receiving emergency calls on field burns gone awry. On late afternoons, my father would zip out into the countryside and douse out the flames that fell onto brush properties that caught the small licks of fire from the burning lands beside them. He would come home after I was already asleep, and I would wait up for him but pretend to be asleep when he came to check on me. And I would breathe in as my room would fill with the smell of smoke and brush fire before my father would creep out and shut the door behind him.

"So the talent scout is clapping and clapping and yelling wildly in front of the clown's white frame. Looking surprised himself, the clown's ghost says, "It's a neat trick, alright, but I—.""

"Wait." Vic stops me. "Do they even have talent scouts anymore?"

BUT I CAN ONLY DO IT ONCE

Hands Like Birds on Strings

[Thursday, 4 September 2003, 23; low-key lighting, single fresnel, white light; 30-degree camera angle downward, close-up]

Before the show starts, Crawford taps his fingers together, points to the screen, and mutters, "I heard somewhere that she's saving for a cochlear implant."

The deaf girl—the one from Watterman Hall; it has to be her because who else could it be?—pretends to be asleep for us at the start of tonight's show, for whomever's watching and paid up. Her hands traipse down from her face and the locks of her rust-tinged hair, laid out and styled in curls, to below her black sheets. We see the traces of soft musculature under the dark sheen of the silk, the movements in rhythm and out of it at the same time, and we turn the sound on our monitors all the way up so we can listen for noises we once heard on old VHS cassettes in our parents' bedrooms or DVDs stashed away in our older cousins' closets.

The sheets inch down slowly, and this is when Monroe, the skater who lives down in 4A, claims he can see her "History of Western Civilization" textbook on the corner of her nightstand. We look for it in the feed, our necks craning closer to the screen, and there it is, *After Rome, Volume I,* the corner dipping into the light just past her bare shoulder. As someone wonders out loud if we'll see the deaf girl in class tomorrow, a sound bursts forth from her— *the sound*—a cry, a small trombone of catharsis, and the show ends just past a quarter to midnight. Monroe excuses himself immediately to the room he shares with Crawford, who stays behind for contraband beer.

Mornings, we stare as the deaf girl writes notes in class, as she preps notes for our shared Organic Chemistry exams, her pen shading the same diamond-shaped hexane rings onto her notepads as our professor makes on the whiteboard. Her dark, russet hair falls to her left side so we can't see what she's musing over or nodding about, but we watch her interpreter's hands whip in circles and lines next to her since they're two of the only things moving in the lecture hall.

In the afternoons, she is with us in Physiology, scratching out the citric acid cycle while we stare at the board with her, dreaming of the day when we won't have to know this by heart, of the years long past a medical residency or a PhD or maybe just even getting through these first four years so we can market pharmaceuticals and go on vacations to Cozumel. And in the early evenings, when some of the others have their Computer Science labs, she's there, too, and we wonder what her major is.

When she walks by us on the campus sidewalks, she's not the same girl we see on the computer screens. We step over the etched names of the alumni from years past on our way to the practice labs, and she's there with us, clipping along in her sandals and jeans and next to the boy her age who follows her to class. Out here, in the sunlight, her lips aren't tamped with the paint she wears for the videos online. The mascara's gone, and the pale foundation and thin eyeliner are muted. If we look closely, we can see the pock marks of whatever acne she's had in the past all gone now, taken away by strong cleansers or pills.

We watch her in the food courts, her and her interpreter as they eat, always silently, save for their hands, which dart over, into, and around themselves like dragonflies, light reflected and glinting off the metal forks at their fingertips. And on some nights, we're there with her, too, with both of them sometimes, our credit cards charged and our monitors on, tuned to the deaf girl on the camera.

The show is always different, but the ending is always the same. A guttural moan, a crescendo into what sounds like the music of pain, unflinching, untainted by the chords of anyone else's pleasure, ever, and this is what keeps us in our rooms on Thursday nights, our wallets out and the doors to our rooms shut against visitors and whomever might not be watching the show like we are.

[Thursday, 23 October 2003; butterfly lighting, multi-source lamps, soft light; 15-degree camera angle downward, mid shot]

The fade-in illuminates the screen like a universe exploding. The light meter on whatever DSLR she's using adjusts down onto the outline of her white kimono at the rear, and we start to see the soft edges of her frame, her pale legs, the contrast of her dark hair draped around her neck like a curtain. The show moves from the over-the-shoulder view to a three-quarter turn, and then a profile shot before she settles into a quarter turn, which is where most of the show stays. The audience, we know, will perch until the fade-out, until the animal sound of a yawn-drowned yell belts out from her, until she's finished, or until we are.

"Have you seen the deaf girl?" is a question we hear in the bars, and the boys will always ask the question to each other, to their friends visiting from other campuses or to other freshmen they've just met. And then those will be the plans for whatever Thursday evening the question's asked: go back to the room terminal, pay for the "11th Hour" streaming fee—her name for the entertainment—or just browse through her galleries of stills from the video feeds if money is tight that week. But most everyone we know stays in on Thursday evenings or goes out drinking early. We make plans to be back at a reasonable hour, when the deaf girl refreshes her page, puts up a new short film, and then makes however much money we send her online. Crawford, who works as a weight room attendant down at the rec, says he's thinking about talking to her in person, asking her if she'll set up a subscription plan for a flat fee. The reason, he says, is because he's always losing his credit card and his room key in the nooks of his gym bag.

At lunch one day, Pulaski, a Comp Sci brat, tells us he remembers when she first started last year. Someone buys him food for the audience with him, and we sit in the oily clouds from all the fried entrees, listening to the story of the freshman on scholarship who hosted her first site on the school's servers.

He takes a drink of his soda and says, "Everyone got 100MB for their own webpages, you know?" and a few of us nod our heads. Crawford's old page is loaded with inspirational quotes from stage actors and bodybuilders. Monroe, who's also the bassist for a jam band called Toad Suck, uses his to promote the local concert scene and to sell t-shirts and logo patches, although no one's bought a thing from him since the start of the semester.

"But here's the genius of the first page she started here," Pulaski says. "She went and loaded the thing up with banners and click-through ads to other, real porn sites. Might've made only a cent or two off each one of those clicks, but that adds up. And I guarantee she made enough off it to pay for that site upgrade off the university servers."

Monroe asks, "So she's a sophomore now?"

And Pulaski nods between bites of spaghetti the cafeteria workers have drenched in peanut oil. He says, "But, man, that site? Her starter? Now that was a thing of beauty."

Not many of us use our webpage slots, and those who do only use it to test out the HTML tags they've learned about in their "Introduction to Computer Science" electives. But we check out hers. The banners on her old site, the one she was given with her email address when she enrolled, are still there, but a link to her new page is featured right there in the middle of the old one. The click-through link is a photo of the girl in profile, venous-red hair shining out past sepia tones, a streak of her body in motion and a reminder of the digital f-stop that wasn't fast enough to catch her as she moved.

[Thursday, 6 November 2003; Rembrandt lighting, halogen lamp with single overhead fresnel; 15-degree angle downward, multiple cuts between mid to quarter-turn, medium close-up shots]

The deaf girl doesn't post a video every Thursday night, but she maintains traffic through gallery stills on the nights she doesn't. She uploads the photos for free, available for viewing and downloading sometime after 11pm. There are men on campus with CD-Rs and hard drives full of her, captured and waiting to be watched again and again at their convenience, like the stills from last week's feed of her showing off a lace and pencil-line set from Victoria's Secret she must have purchased in the last month. We remember how, in the final jump cut to the third set of underwear, however, the cloth stayed on. We watched her move the fabric back and forth, touching it and the flesh below with the tips of her fingers until the material was soaked through. We remember how Garland, the dorm's kleptomaniac, perched over the crowd we made around Pulaski's 28-inch monitor, fresh from a cigarette break outside, him whispering under his breath, "It's what we're not seeing, you know? It's burlesque."

And we waited for the end, for the sound. That night, it took us by aural surprise: a shriek of the letter 'e,' a long vowel of what might have been panic had it not ended in the uplift of a brief sigh, a drop of the legs to the duvet, a fade.

Pulaski, who's taking Ritalin and learning C++ on the weekends, tells us she's here on scholarship, with free room and board, and, because of the additional stipends, she's making money off of school already. He tells us the deaf girl started small with the allocation requests. A doorbell light for her dorm room. A video relay service that the university had to pay for anyway once the ADA saw she'd made the request, and so on. But he tells us that she's stopped making allocation requests out of her scholarship funds.

She's sitting on them for something big, he says, but he won't tell us what he's thinking.

"Maybe it's for surgery or for a boob job," Garland says, clipping his toenails on his ledge. Below us, cars drive between the football stadium and its parking garages. We see drunk people stumbling back to their apartments. "Or maybe that's where she gets the money for her interpreter."

"Look, I don't know how he gets paid," Pulaski clips back, "but that's not it."

The translator is tall, taller than she is, and lanky. The thin skin on his fingers stretches out like webbing on a spider's limbs. Small tufts of dark hair the color of his sideburns run over his knuckles. When he signs for her, sitting next to her or at the front of the class with his eyes fixed on the deaf girl and no one else, his hands swoop like fighter planes, spin like he's working on a puzzle box only he can touch.

[Thursday, 20 November 2003; split lighting, single fluorescent light source, 75-degree downward angle, overhead, medium close-up]

He is her prop. An object of hers, like a loofah or a bottle of shampoo she's brought with her into the shower. She grabs his neck, or she pulls him toward her for a rough kiss, or she pushes his head down to between her legs, holds him there like a steering wheel, like a rugby ball in the middle of a play. We watch his fingers run over her breasts, the globes of her ass. We pay money to watch her guide him into the places we can't see but desperately want to. We watch her stare up at the camera she's hoisted onto the rim of a bathroom stall somewhere on campus, smiling like she knows we're watching her live, slamming into the translator like he's been affixed to the shower wall with suction cups and pain.

Monroe remarks the next morning, "I appreciate that editing. She cut out before he came. Nobody needs to hear that." And we laugh.

"I'm going to say he's certified," Crawford pipes up. "Must've gone through a whole slew of tests if he wanted to get paid by the state to interpret for her."

We see the interpreter sometimes without the deaf girl, walking on campus like he's off to his own classes and late for them. He wears Chuck Taylors and his backpack over one shoulder. He carries an old DiscMan with him, listens to music on bulky headphones and dodges the questions of the boys on campus.

"My great aunt was deaf," Crawford explains. "Had a guy who went with her to community theater sometimes and signed along with the dialogue. Got state certified and all, except I don't think she was fucking him."

And so like her, we treat the interpreter when he's out by himself just like she does: as someone we might see in their videos sometimes, a useful tool for the star of the show, an out-of-the-spotlight extra with no lines.

Tonight, though, they walk together to the computer labs for class, apart and pacing together down the concrete lane. They look like a couple that's been fighting in the close quarters of a vehicle, the disgust between them a passenger.

"If it was serious," Garland claims, "we'd have seen them holding hands sometime." But we know what they have is serious, even if it's not love or lust, and we leave it at that. Friends fight, too, and so do costars.

Pulaski and Crawford, who've been drinking on the lawn outside the IT building, rush back with news once the dining halls are closed.

"We couldn't see the device when she was on her way to class," Pulaski puffs out, exhausted from his run, "but there it is!"

"Check out her hair," Crawford says, who's drunk but in shape, his fingers in pantomime around his ear. And there she is in the dorm hallways, the one side of her head shaved down to the skin. She's shed herself of the translator, too, who we'd normally see perched in the corner of her room with a book.

[Thursday, 6 December 2003; flat lighting, single forward halogen positioned over camera, level close-up shot, repositioned to 30 degrees downward angle]

At the beginning of the show tonight, she signs to us. Or not to us, rather, but to her few deaf viewers with a level of access the majority is missing out on right now. We watch her hands flip over each other in a language we can't read, and there's a joy we haven't seen before, a girl who smiles at us in her unbuttoned mandarin top, whose fingers dart over, into, and around themselves like birds on strings. Between what we read as paragraphs, she punctuates the end of each block of text with another unclasped loop of her shirt, and we look to the index and middle fingers of her right hand, which have formed a drooping 'V,' a snake's fangs at the end of her palms, which she uses to strike at the back of her right ear. We don't notice what she's pointing to until the second time she taps the spot with her fingers, and there it is: the cochlear implant.

And Crawford crosses his arms in self-satisfaction, nestling his hands into the warmth of his armpits, says, "I told you. See?" He sips his beer and raises it to her face on the screen, says, "Well, good for her, I guess."

She signs to us, to the camera, before tilting it down. She wears a striped pair of gray-toned underwear tonight that matches the brassiere she's unclasped now that her top's off. And for the first time this semester, the air in the room feels heavy, thick with boys streaked in acne and sweat and watching something different, all of us tense with the implausible thought that she might now be listening back.

Crawford rubs his eyes and checks his watch, says in his delta drawl, "I read about those implants. What they do is they put a receiver under her skin and dig it down into the cochlea. They bypass the inner ear directly. Amazing stuff, you know?" He tosses popcorn into his mouth. The dorm hallways smell like boys' feet and the fake butter rolling around in his microwaveable bag. "And that bit there?" he asks, pointing at the brown crescent moon of plastic wrapped around the deaf girl's cartilage. His fingertip greases the screen. "That's her microphone. That particular model, I'm guessing, listens for voices and words, shoots it through that transmitter cord. Taps it through the electrodes on the other side. Want some?" He shakes the loose cloud of burst kernels at us, but no one reaches in.

We watch the deaf girl's legs rise up and crease at the knees. We watch what we've paid to, at the motion of the soft folds of her. Mostly we stare at the side of her head, where the tufts of hair are starting to come back in and grow over the plastic. Near the end, as the video countdown drops into the last minute, we lean forward, waiting for her sound, the sound of abandonment and release that can't be fit into consonants. But the sound tonight is a squeak of a surprise, clipped off by its own awareness, an *eep!* of volume and a laugh from her pale throat we've never heard before.

She waves goodbye to the camera, fades to black onscreen, and none of us moves back to our rooms as we've done the rest of the semester. Crawford, arms still folded, says, "Cheers to the deaf girl." He says it soundly and finally, like he's sending her soul off into the night.

[Thursday, 20 December 2003; "Error 404"]

Her site is down, gone and missing from the host, but she's there with us in Physiology, leaning forward in her chair to read the professor's lips anytime he makes a class announcement from his corner lectern. Her interpreter's off in his own exams, as absent from her side as the videos and photo galleries on her site. We've barely seen him since the cold snap has come. The pair of them move around campus in wide circles that never touch.

Pulaski meets us afterward near the loading docks to the labs, smoking in the minutes before his Advanced Logic final. "Her old site's down, too," he says, confirming what we already know. "The click-throughs, the links, the page script: it's all gone. If you haven't saved her stills or video captures by this point, you're out of luck." But some of us have, and we try to guess who among us besides Pulaski has a spindle of CDs with her face and her moan written in laser on them.

We watch as she leaves at the end of exams, her parents in the front seat of their champagne-colored sedan, she in the back. Her interpreter has come to wish the family goodbye, and the deaf girl's mother hugs his thin frame hard, her arms falling over his bony shoulders in waves. We watch as the girl who has appeared on our monitors trundles down the hill from campus, not bothering to say goodbye to the boy, though maybe she already has in some other fashion. We wonder about what's been said between them, if anything, and what might ever be said again.

To celebrate the end of the semester that night, we follow the street down and away from campus to the bars, to the taprooms where the townies let us come in, drink, shut up, and listen to the jukebox as it plays records from Patsy Cline and George Jones. The woman pouring drafts has a Sailor Jerry outline of an anchor on her deltoid, with the word "Steady" in cursive below it, and then Monroe mutters, "I'm finally ready, I think. I am ready for a tattoo." And that's enough for us to settle the check and follow him up the road to the only parlor open this time of night.

Someone nudges him on the cobblestones, almost makes him trip, asking, "What's it going to be?" And Monroe smiles and says, "Her," pointing toward the lights of campus. "I want her over my heart, every pixel of her," and that's enough for us to yell and clap him on the back and make offers to pay for part of the session fee on his behalf.

He'll regret this in the morning, maybe, we joke, but there's a pull in his walk that makes us hope he'll look down at the results and nod and drive for his home over the winter break with a smile there. And when the tattoo artist sizes us up, tells everyone but Monroe and Crawford to wait in the lobby, we do as we're told, and we collect $20 bills together before passing them to the artist behind the register. After Monroe settles on a design—a front shot illustration, her arms and hands busy signing in front of her chest, from a time before the implant—we sober up and flip through the sketch books and the albums of yellowing Polaroids from the parlor's clients, and we listen to Crawford's updates from behind the rear wall of the shop.

"He's doing it," he dispatches, whispering like a spy. "He's really doing it."

We turn a page of the newest book of client photos. A patch of a student's deltoid blazes out our school mascot, a warthog with a single tusk jutting out of his lips, and someone near the door makes the rutting, grunting sound the football stands fill with each Saturday.

Pulaski mumbles on his way off to sleep in the corner, "Endorphins are probably kicking in about now. It's the body's response to pain. Good for Monroe." We turn the page to see a set of angel's wings, black and shaded into feathers on the photograph, and we let Pulaski doze under the sound of the needle in the back.

"Head and face are all done," Crawford says later, checking in from around the corner. "Not a bad likeness, really."

We turn another album page. We listen to Monroe make a quick yelp from the chair, and then Crawford's away from us, back by his side. Below us, we look down at the photo of a client's soft spine and the two inked rows of girls from the children's book, Madeline, trailing in formation behind Miss Clavelle and the outline of the Eiffel Tower in the background.

We turn the page again, listening for the buzz of the needle on Monroe's skin from somewhere, and then, to our surprise, the chest plate of a girl we think we've seen before somewhere shines back up at us from the album.

"Is that—?" is all Garland can get out before we stop talking.

Her sternum is captured in a close-up, with flat lighting shining from only the flash of the camera, and we see what she's spent the last of her scholarship money on.

"What?" Crawford asks, tripping back into view and turning the album. "I want to see."

And from Pulaski, yawning and twisting now, and who's woken up for the occasion, "Oh."

The photo of the tattoo on the page is of a wave form, black ink on pale skin, an intricate sound graph measured by an oscilloscope and made into a tattoo. It jumps in precise, sinusoidal lines from the top of the pendulum of her right breast over the top of her left. It leaps erratically, an audio signature of something none of us can understand or read, save for the frequency at its peaks.

The ink on her skin, the videos recorded and broadcast out into the world: these are what we'll remember most about college. Someday, when our wives or girlfriends will ask about our time spent as undergrads, we'll lie and tell them we have the fondest memories about the late-night cram sessions for Vertebrate Morphology, or about tailgating in the giant bowl of the parking lot, underneath the stretch of the dorms and the fraternity houses in a row. We won't tell them about the deaf girl, though, or about the money we spent to watch her under the lights.

Snuff Film

Antennae fly up and off the top of the United States Nuclear Regulatory Commission's office towers, each of them dotted red by aircraft warning lights that pulse in halos through the mist and rain tonight. Conference rooms line the floors of the towers below, where video link sessions run over the building's dedicated OC-48 lines, all the way down through to the second-floor auditorium, the small cafeteria just off the lobby, and the busy IT center in the basement. Tonight, a janitor empties the waste baskets below the conference table of the sub-basement "war room," as some of the onsite technicians call it. She polishes the oversized wooden table in the middle of the room, only in the spots where the veneer peeks out, between unkempt piles of paper and sleeping laptops, and then she leaves. Above the chaos, circuit monitors stationed over the table spit out broadcasts from various news stations with the volume turned down low, along with a half-dozen live and muted feeds from Russellville, Arkansas: exterior shots of a cooling tower next to an emptied parking lot, an overhead view of rows upon rows of exhaust piping, multiple angles on a pair of squat reactor units, a single wide shot out toward a moonlit lake in the distance. Save for the basement janitor, most of the office employees here in Maryland have left for the evening, and they aren't there to witness the new, small movement on the monitors now, where there hasn't been any in the last few days: two people, an elderly couple, stepping carefully into focus.

For the last week, node access from the CCTV system down at Arkansas Nuclear One has been the sole broadcast through the USNRC's new offices. Optical networks relay the images globally: to the plant's owner, Entergy Nuclear, down in New Orleans; to the Commission's new building in North Bethesda, just over a thousand miles northeast of the accident site; to the International Atomic Energy Agency's regional offices in Toronto. Everyone is tuned in, but no one is watching when they should be.

"Happy Tuesday, Bethesda. And if the regional director's not gone to bed yet: to you, too, Toronto," says the old woman, the skin of her cheeks stretched into a smile. She says this into the lens on the robot that's been sent into the exposure zone, goes back to the binder on the desk in front of her after only a moment. "My watch is still working, so it's just turned midnight there, correct?"

A rustling can be heard in the corner. Fabric moves; an old office chair squeaks.

"It looks like we've been discovered, Joseph," the woman says. "Finally."

From the corner, the old man with her lifts his gloved hand toward the robot, waves, lets it drop back down to his side.

"And guten morgen to you, too, Vienna," she says back at the camera. Then, after a moment, "Actually, if any of you at the IAEA headquarters are watching right now, I take that back. This isn't good. This is actually pretty bad. You should probably wake up the North Americans."

The old man in the corner lifts his hand again, making a thumbs-down sign this time, and then adjusts his face mask before plopping his arm back down into his lap.

The robot's boom swivels around the dimly lit area slowly on its servos: down to the floor, up at the ceiling, zooming in next to the dark space beyond the door of whatever room the elderly couple has occupied. It pulls back to readjust, and then the camera tracks slowly toward the black hole below the EXIT sign.

"I wouldn't go down there if I were you," says the woman. "You've got the railing and then the steps, and then right below that is a hotspot. Dosimeter's reading spikes of anywhere between 2,000 and 3,000 millisieverts per hour, and I'm going to bet you're not shielded enough for that, are you?"

Whoever's controlling the robot stops it in its tracks, zooms into the darkness again, pauses, and then swivels back around to show the full expanse of the room.

It's a control center, white-paneled and lined with terminals in two rows in front of a bank of monitors and switches up on the wall. The screens are all black and so are the smaller monitors on the panels, save for a few blinking red lights. Above the man and the woman is an emergency lamp that floods them brightly and then cuts out every so often. The camera, equipped with a night-vision function, struggles to keep up with the changes, burning white-hot each time the light on the wall flickers back.

"Told you," says the woman in the chair. She clears her throat and studies the manual in front of her as intently as the robot's lens studies her.

—

The nuclear disaster in Arkansas has been the biggest story of the week for most of the news channels. In Maryland, a screen tuned to CNN recaps how the earthquake stemming from Oklahoma crashed toward the New Madrid seismic zone somewhere in West Central Arkansas, where it overloaded the river and Lake Dardanelle.

Stock analysts on Bloomberg and Sky News have raised the loudest alarms—"Soybean futures are down," they've cried, talking about the soon-to-be irradiated crops in the Arkansas delta—and, in between commercials, bullet-point timelines detailing how workers at the nuclear plant had just enough time to shut down the fission loads in the main reactor before they were evacuated, but that the earthquake and the flooding together had disabled the plant's emergency generators.

"There's still no power to control and operate the cooling pumps," the CNN correspondent explains. His taped piece contains shots from a hilltop overlooking the concave tower, his blue rain jacket whipping in the wind and the light rain of earlier that afternoon. He looks up to the sky with a pained expression on his face, like the drops themselves are full of heat and poison. "We know there's been a meltdown in the main reactor as a result," he continues, "and a blowout from a hydrogen leak into the air, and then there's the fallout on the ground that's pouring into the Arkansas River." He finishes his report breathlessly while, downstream, the population of Little Rock continues to empty out in a steady rush of exhaust fumes and panic.

"Here, sweetie," the woman says. The robot watches as she hoists a lined blue hood up over the man's head. The rest of him is already fitted into a bulky suit of some type of rubber and blue plastic. A filter mask with two ports juts out at the mouth, just below an open rectangle of gray film the user can peek out through. The camera zooms in as the woman gently unclasps something near the man's mouth, whispering, "I don't think you need this right now," and then a smaller surgical mask falls to the floor next to the couple. They share a familiarity of movements, something decades in the making between partners.

The rover's operator adjusts the depth and focus of the lens, but it can't catch the blocked motions of the man and the woman with her back turned. Its relayed feed of the control room picks up the rise and fall of the old man's breathing, though, and it watches as the woman's husband strokes her arm gently with his hand. She turns to look at the camera.

"Y'all are going to need better suits to deal with the amount of gamma pouring out of here," she says, tapping somewhere on the shell of the robot's shielding. She looks down at the rubberized fabric of her own ill-fitting suit. "These old DuPont rigs we found in the emergency lockers are fine for the alpha and beta rays, but five bucks says there's not much of a boron layer left in the face masks. Expiration date's coming up on three years now, it looks like. And for what it's worth, you cheap bastards, I'm surprised we're still standing right now. I'm nauseated and my throat's sore. Vision's getting difficult, too, now that I think about it." She flicks her wrist at the lens. "If you could turn away for a second?"

She starts to strip down to her bra and leggings, and this is when the camera swivels to the left. If nothing else, the rover's operator at least has some sense of modesty.

The robot's boom droops down toward the floor of the control center for a few minutes, and then the sound of Velcro being pulled apart is heard offscreen, then the distinct rip of heavy-duty tape. The camera risks a quick look back over to the right, and there's the old woman standing up as tall as she can, with her own hood tipped over the back of her suit. She looks like the figure of a plastic Lego astronaut come to life, her face stern and set in the pulsing lights of the control center.

Just after midnight in Maryland, a pre-taped segment on Bloomberg relays a found-footage compilation of what's happening at Arkansas Nuclear One.

Still photos of the flooded disaster site and the rough barricades that've been stocked around the nuclear plant and the exterior perimeter of Russellville itself.

A recording made by a hiker's shaking handheld camera. He yells as the ground trembles around him during the earthquake, catching footage of the water of Lake Dardanelle pouring over the banks toward the slope and down toward the cooling tower.

Surreptitious video of National Guard troops milling about on the yellow stripes of a two-lane road. A highway marker next to them shows the outline of the Arkansas state map, with a black "22" in the middle.

A phone's camera trained on a laptop that's streaming one of Arkansas Tech's webcams nearby. The streetlights around the Russellville campus are still running, still bright in the nighttime, but all the cars are gone from the university, and there aren't any students on the quad. Blips of small animals sprinting across the grass, then a voice off to the right asks, "Are those bobcats?"

—

"As this is probably our last call-in," the woman on the feed says, "I'm just going to come out and say it. To the members of the International Atomic Energy Agency and to you bastards from the state nuclear commission who didn't shut down the plants after 2003, and, hell—if this gets leaked to the public, fine—to the fracking assholes in Oklahoma who set this whole thing off: Like I said, this is bad."

The woman pulls a heavy blue glove onto her left hand and locks it into the metal frame at the cuff of the suit. The rover watches as she wraps thick tape around the fitting and continues.

"Now pay attention. Since your machines keep getting fried when they're sent in, Joseph over there and I are here to close what I'm pretty sure is an open vent in the containment building and then lock the nitrogen feed back in. Which I'm guessing is why there's still so much fallout past the first reactor vessel." She looks over the camera toward a point in the distance we can't see. "If you hear a big 'kaboom,' by the way, the hydrogen was still leaking out. Sorry if we leave a mess."

The man in the azure suit claps his hands together in a muffled tympani and then shakes his hands and fingers out in a mock explosion. For the first time since the robot made contact with the couple, the old man can be heard to make a noise: "Ka-hoom!"

The woman smirks. "Sweetheart, you are too much." She turns her attention back to the robot's lens. "But your real problem is getting power back to the stations. The batteries over there are dead, right? And I'm going to take it that you can't get the backup generators in gear after the flooding?"

The robot's operator seems to hesitate here. After too long a moment, the rover's boom shakes up and down in a "yes."

"That's what I thought," the woman says, matter-of-factly. "Oh, and you've got a low-level fire over in Unit 2. I don't know if it's eating power cables or what over there, but that's probably what's making that ribbon of black smoke in the sky, if that's helpful."

In the slightest possible shimmying of the lens up and down, the robot appears to shrug. Like the operator is in agreement with the woman but is powerless to do anything, the camera does its best impression of sympathy.

This will all be over soon, it seems to say.

In Maryland, the BBC livestream on one of the monitors switches from a report on Canada's negotiations with OPEC to a "Breaking News" overlay. A styled desk anchor checks her notes and the teleprompter before nodding, saying, "Concerning the flooding and containment failure of the Arkansas Nuclear One power plant, we're being told that two individuals have just breached the protective barriers at the site and have entered the plant's control center. The footage seen here is provided by a source with the International Atomic Energy Agency." Onscreen, the woman is seen helping Joseph stand up from his chair. She smooths down the Velcro and tape on the back of the man's blue suit exterior, steadying him before trudging out of view. Below the footage, a chyron on the screen reads: "U.S.: Trespassers spotted inside AR Nuclear 1."

Within minutes, the IAEA footage is picked up by CNN, Al Jazeera, NDTV, NHK, and CGTN, each of them listing the cycled video as "Breaking News." Within a half-hour, links to the news stations' stories on the event are circulated through social media: WeChat and QQ, Twitter and Reddit. At the bottom of a set of comments on the r/DaughtersOfTheAtom subreddit, a small exchange takes place:

> [MaryCurEEE] * 10m
> Five bucks says that's Maggie St. James.
>> [RabbitHvtch83] * 7m
>> Who?
>>> [MaryCurEEE] * 6m
>>> Used to work for the Tennessee Valley Authority in plant design and regulation. I cite her a lot in my dissertation. Didn't know she was still alive until I saw an interview with her last year.
>>>> [-^-Splitter-^-] * 3m
>>>> link?

The BBC adds in another "Breaking News" overlay before showing the next segment of video feed from the plant. It shows the man and the woman in the muted blue protective suits moving slowly toward the rover and an exit point beyond. The robot with the attached camera rolls forward on its tracks, swivels, and then bolts to catch up with them. The couple's bulky protective suits slow them down a bit, but they walk evenly, measuredly, as they trudge between buildings on the concrete strip next to the lake. Their steps toward the containment building are slow and lumbering, and the robot seems to pace behind them like an obedient dog.

"On three," Maggie says. The St. Jameses grab onto the rungs of a metal wheel lock outside the containment building doors.

"One," she says, and Joseph nods.

The rover looks up at them from its full height of four feet.

"Two."

It turns its neck toward the oversized, locked doors to its left, as though it's realizing right now what's happening. Without power being fed to the compound, there's nothing to help the couple open the exterior doors to the containment building, save for the manual system backup, and that requires some elbow grease.

"Three."

And the robot retreats from the giant doors, unsure of what will pour out of them.

In Maryland, another monitor relays a muted broadcast of KARK, a news channel in Little Rock showing a live helicopter feed of the traffic jam on I-40 East, as cars continue pouring out from the capital toward the Tennessee border and away from the poisoned Lake Dardanelle and its flowing river. From where the helicopter is perched, it's nothing but a red swarm of brake lights in winding columns toward Memphis and not a single pair of headlights going west.

Inch by inch at the wheel, the door has opened foot by foot next to the St. Jameses. From the outside, the containment building looks like a great cylinder of concrete and metal, looming over the couple like a giant can of soda. Slowly and carefully, as if it's hoping there's room enough for it, too, the robot's operator guides the vehicle behind the elderly couple, easing up its speed as it shuffles in through the doors.

Inside the towering structure, a ring of orange emergency lights around the circumference of the floor comes to life. The visibility's minimal at first, like it's gotten the signal that a guest of importance has entered the room. The camera moves toward one of the lights and zooms in, centering on a dark shield of film covering the single bulb at its center.

The rover's servos spin together now, moving the machine forward toward the pooled steam and vapor in the middle of the building. From somewhere behind the gigantic concrete pylon there, the gases whirl and lift and fall and repeat—a rough beast of poison that slouches down to the ground and sticks to the walls and tumbles over and over, condensing into water droplets that stream into rivulets on the concrete floor below.

From the direction of the St. Jameses, a sharp alarm goes off, and the robot's treads whip around in time to see a flash from the old woman's dosimeter.

"Stop!" she yells, breathing hard still. "Look, whatever happens with the vent and the nitrogen line and everything else, I'm sorry if we get stuck here. You can pull us out someday once it's safe."

She pats the top of the robot's head again, at a point somewhere above the lens, and the boom jostles in the bright lights of the containment building. She and Joseph walk toward the water vapor as it pours out from the lined wall, and, as the robot moves to follow, Maggie leans over and lets the rover's optics read the LCD display on the dosimeter. The millisieverts of measured radiation dash up and down on the counter, and an alarm goes off each time it spikes until she unhooks it and throws the device into the corner.

"You have to stay here!" Maggie yells through the rubberized suit. "Your circuits will fry if you get any closer, and then you won't know if we've vented it or not. Get it?"

So the robot stays still. From its stationary point, the boom's movable neck follows the St. Jameses as they trudge to the open space behind the giant pillar of concrete.

And then, like a Greek tragedy, the violence happens just off-stage.

The **BBC** desk anchor stops her recap, stares at the monitor in front of her, motionless, waits for something to happen.

"Over here, sweetheart," can be heard offscreen somewhere.

Above the **USNRC**'s war room table in Maryland, the anchor is speaking to anyone watching and to no one. "Are we watching this happen?" she asks. "Are we really? I mean, is this Fukushima all over again?"

After a minute's worth of nothing, a heavy clang of metal on metal can be heard, then the scraping noise of what sounds like a lid being screwed onto a glass jar.

No one is sitting around the conference table in Maryland to imagine the worst: the radiated vapor being piped into Maggie and Joseph St. Jameses' hooded faces, the **DNA** of their cells being twisted and rendered out of proper function, the nausea overtaking them, the organ failure. No one is there tonight to plan what to do with their bodies until months or years later, when the rovers' shielding can be corrected and reengineered to function, when Arkansas Nuclear One can be disassembled safely, and when people might return to the middle of the state.

Slowly, though, and almost imperceptibly onscreen, the steam tapers off and dissipates, the last of it falling to the floor, bouncing playfully, wisping away, finally, like ghosts caught on film.

And then there they are: two suits of wet azure from around the corner, stumbling in the heavy protective gear and back toward the camera, one holding the arm of the other for support.

The figure in blue on the left crumples forward toward the rover, heavy with sound. A retching noise from behind the plastic hood. A gargling, wet-filled noise, and then a thick, syrupy cough.

The figure pulls the tape and Velcro away from his hood, unzips the clasp surrounding the bottom of the plastic shell. It's Joseph, and as he rips the hood away from his head, his shoulders droop, and the retching noise goes to full volume, a thin, yellow gruel now streaming from his mouth and nostrils onto the ground.

"Oh, sweetheart," Maggie says. "Oh, my sweet, wonderful man, I'm sorry."

If someone were watching in the USNRC's offices tonight, they'd see what Joseph had hidden under his mask this entire time. There are two holes where the bottom of his jaw should be. Two lines of fresh sutures below what's left of a bottom lip, and a plastic tracheotomy port that juts out from just below the wounds. A swath of raw and roughshod skin below it that looks like it's gone through radiation therapy. From one of the suture lines, a fresh welt of blood is beginning to weep through from all the coughing, and vomit still clings to what's left of Joseph's jawline as he lifts his head.

The rover stares down at Joseph St. James as he struggles up to his knees, rolls forward on its rough treads as though it means to help.

"C'mon, old timer," Maggie says. "The chemo last year didn't kill you, and fixing the vent hasn't killed you, either." She hoists her husband to his feet and starts walking them toward the giant metal doors. "We aren't staying here, though, and we sure as hell aren't dying here now that the vent line's been patched."

In the orange light of the containment building, Maggie St. James and her husband walk below a burned-out EXIT sign. Before they leave, though, she turns to the robot, her hood swiveling with her, and yells out, "Y'all have so much work ahead of you."

The rover starts to follow on its treads but then stops when the engineer does, watching her now as she gives the thumbs-up sign and stumbles out and away.

"Good luck!" she shouts into the night.

For whatever reason—dead batteries, circuits burned crisp by radiation, orders from the operator not to leave—the robot stays put, its camera unmoving as it tracks the St. Jameses lurching away. In the darkness, it loses sight of them as they turn a corner.

Above the polished table in the North Bethesda basement, the BBC feed cuts back to the desk anchor, who breathes for a moment and finishes her OPEC report. CNN, Bloomberg, and CGTN each cut to commercial while the news ticker restarts on NHK. Above it all, the janitor in Maryland shuts down the lights in the lobby's foyer, rides down to the basement for her final once-over for the night.

Down in the war room, though, an action sequence starts up again on one of the exterior security cameras at the flood site: a sound of servos and wheels spinning in the nighttime, of treads rumbling over slick pavement, a fixed shot of the rover gearing up to full speed again, moving forward now to an unknown point. At the top of the feed is a white, white moon, a burning emblem on a dark field, and the robot is seen pushing forward on the road out of Arkansas Nuclear One.

On another fixed spot in the CCTV series from Russellville, lights still dot the background of the hills around Lake Dardanelle. Somewhere up on the road going out, a deer dashes across the highway, pauses at the median, and then leaps out again into the groves around a now-abandoned gas station, safe now that the two lurching figures have passed out of view of the shot.

The monitor beaming out the NHK news ticker brightens up again. The chyron on the screen explains that the live video capture being seen is courtesy of the IAEA's Toronto offices.

Whatever stored energy the robot has left is being used to race along the road and catch up with the St. Jameses. Its treads lurch the chassis forward at an uneven pace, drawing power from a fickle battery. Under the clear moonlight, the engineer and her husband's suits gleam black as one of them pulls the other along.

"Hello?" says Maggie. She turns her ears toward the sound behind them, but she doesn't spin her head to look. Like Joseph, she's removed her own protective hood. It droops behind her like a spent parachute, and she trudges along with its weight at her back.

The camera stops, but the St. Jameses don't, so the rover fires back up again, trailing slowly now and matching their pace.

The couple doesn't turn back, but the camera's microphone picks up their words anyway: "It's just a short walk to the Whataburger," Maggie says. "Right down the road here?" If Joseph has said anything—could say anything—there's no one else to hear it.

Half-glancing back at the camera every few feet now, Maggie's words slur out. "It'll come back to you. Popped up after the plant came in. Got that 1950s throwback feel to it. Lots of chrome and faded photos of grilled patties and hot fries, remember?"

Next to her, Joseph's pace starts to slow as his head droops. In the cresting distance, bright lights start to swivel and oscillate. Emergency services, the police, the National Guard outpost on the road: It could be any or all of them.

"Why you proposed on our fourth date, you beautiful man, I'll never know," she says, slowing her walk and pointing ahead. For someone who's soaked up an intense number of rads so recently, her breathing isn't as raspy or thin as it should be, although her husband's is. Joseph's pace drops again, down to almost nothing but a shuffle. The beams in front of them expand, casting flickers of light on the steps ahead. He slows, stops, starts again, falters. The man's knees fall to meet the pavement below.

"Like we knew anything about anything," his wife says, chasing a memory down.

The old woman stops, too, just a few feet in front of her husband, turning now toward the camera. Under the moonlight and through the night vision, the lens zooms in on the burn marks that are starting to form on Maggie's skin, like those belonging to Joseph. Red, chapped swaths on the engineer's face that stream down toward her throat like thrush. A map of burned flesh where only the hood has protected her, from the radiation that poured out from the unstable fuel rods of the containment building.

"Just right up here," she says, revving up once more.

Something in her stops, though, catches the light now from the vehicles ahead.

"Oh, sweetheart, we're in trouble now," she says to her husband on the road. "See? They're waiting for us."

On the Rockville Pike in Maryland, in the basement of one of the newest buildings on the strip, a single monitor broadcasts out this moment to no one: of Maggie St. James leaning in toward the unmanned ground vehicle's camera, of the crackle of an AV unit barking demands some 50 yards in front her on the road, of the engineer as she puts her hand over a spot above her heart, a gesture all Southerners know. "We shared a greasy one-pounder that night, an order of fries, and a cola apiece, then you just up and popped the question to me from across the booth? The very idea. But what the hell did we know?"

Under the bright moonlight, in grainy resolution over stretched bandwidth, the rover watches as the old woman slumps down just feet away from the figure on the pavement behind her. The pair of them are as still as the emergency rigs up ahead, unmoving, and now the robot's boom stretches and curls to look for breath in the couple's bodies. It might be there, it might not, but the robot's treads move closer to investigate. The lens zooms in on the woman's chest to look for movement, but there's nothing here. No rise, no fall of gas within the lungs to make them expand and contract. Just a ripple of wind coming off the flooded lake around them. The gust flaps at the layers of the suit, tries its best to inflate the thing like a balloon, up from under the woman's still frame, and it almost succeeds.

92

GHOSTS CAUGHT ON FILM

Heavy Petting

Pity and I were smoking with a pair of sixth graders near the school's lunch dumpsters when the gulls swooped in. We watched the birds pull at the spaghetti that streamed down the rims, remembering how the lunch ladies would fill up the bins each week with uneaten angel hair or fettuccine, how the flocks would dive in for the fresh stuff not ten minutes after.

"Lookit the seagulls!" one of the kids said. When he clapped, the ash on his Newport fell off in a clump.

"Don't say 'seagulls'," I told him. "We live upstate. You see a sea around here? No? Call them 'ring-billed gulls,' then, if you want to get fucking technical. Common as head lice up here."

"You shouldn't cuss, Mr. Fitz," said the kid's friend, scratching his head. He had orange hair, not red. Orange. Bright as Bozo's.

"This here is an employee smoke break, kiddo," I said, laying a hand on Pity's shoulder. "Mr. Fitz gets fifteen minutes of cancer every three hours, no teaching required. Government mandate."

Pity piped in: "And fifteen minutes of quiet."

"But those are seagulls," Bozo started, and then, "Ow!" Because that's when Pity zinged his lit joint at the kid's left cheek. Principal Coach and the school's steroidal Vice Principals didn't mind our janitor's pot stash so long as Pity was the one plunging toilets. Deadly aim, that Pity.

"I said 'quiet'!" yelled Pity, not quiet at all. So the sixth graders trudged back over to recess in a huff. They'd return with their Newports tomorrow, and everything would be just fine again.

"Now that amateur hour's over," Pity said, "we've got demands to discuss."

"Demands?" I said. I thought of my ex-wife, Jan Allen, and her girlfriend, Belinda. I thought of the legal envelope and the unsigned closing contract they'd dropped off with me again on Monday. I'd had enough of demands for the week. "Like what?"

Pity rolled another joint, took a small list out of his shirtsleeve pocket.

"West exit by the band room needs a fire extinguisher," he started. "I can carve out a chunk in the brickwork there, but it ain't up to code otherwise."

"Easy peasy," I said. I dreamed of calling the fire marshal if Coach didn't comply. Red lights and helmets and the wrath of the local hook & ladder on him and everything. "What else?"

"Eighth-grade French needs a Blu-ray player," he continued, "and seventh-grade Geography needs an atlas of Europe with no East or West Germany on it. Just Germany. A big one."

With Pity, it was never 'Mademoiselle Flaneur' or "Mr. Grigsby.' Just the faculty's grades and subjects. Pity could turn anything into ceremony.

"It'd be no more than fifty bucks," Pity explained. He shot out five fingers on his left hand like he was learning to count. "Coach could go for that, no problem."

"It'll be eighty minimum," I told him, our free period almost over. "We'll have to go through central purchasing for it. Gotta find the lowest bid and all that."

Pity shook both hands this time, ten fingers flying now. "Hell, boy, you know damn well Wal-Mart's got the lowest bid. How come we can't ever just buy from the supercenter?"

"It's all invoices and budgets," I said. I left it at that because sometimes I had to. "You done?"

Pity took another puff, and I waved the smoke away. "One more thing," he said.

"Let's have it."

A gull landed on one of the bins next to us. I'd never seen one fish out and eat a meatball before, but here we were.

"You missed it at the meeting last week, but we got to talking," he started. The meatball the gull had picked up was swallowed and out of sight now. But it bulged in the bird's throat now and didn't move.

"Spit it out," I said.

In front of Pity and me, the gull started to dance and panic. It was choking on its spongy find.

"You talking to me or the bird?" Pity asked.

We watched the gull crank its neck up and down as it tried to dislodge the meat.

"You," I said, still watching the thing thrash.

"No more Thursday night football," Pity said. "Please." He kicked the words out of his mouth like he was confessing to something terrible. "School spirit be damned."

In front of us, the gull hit its head on the rim of the dumpster. It clanged back and forth on the edge, hard, but the ball in the middle of its neck stayed stuck.

"This something you all want?" I said.

Pity stepped in front of me. Made eye contact and looked all business.

"We took a vote," he said. Held me by both shoulders like we were slow dancing. A foxtrot or a soft waltz, maybe. Like something Jan Allen and I might have done once.

Behind us, the bird started hitting its head on the plastic lid. In the cafeteria somewhere was a poster showing how to perform the Heimlich maneuver.

"Unanimous decision," he pleaded.

I couldn't see the bird as it fell. Pity was blocking my line of sight, and I wondered if he'd leave a burn mark on my shirt sleeve. But I heard the thing hit the pavement. A soft whump, and then we both turned to confirm something horrible or natural had happened.

"Okay, then," I said. The gull's one exposed eye stared up at nothing and at everything. Above us, a flock of white birds—his friends, maybe?—circled and made plans for noodles and half-eaten bread rolls. "I'll let him know."

On my parade to the Vice Principals' rumpus rooms and Principle Coach's leather-lined office, I thought of the frozen faculty bodies on Thursday nights and got angry. I thought of us standing in the cold, soda-streaked bleachers for two hours each week, cheering on every pissant play the JV squad ran. Five-yard interceptions from the QB to the other team. Views of the ball flying backwards behind the kicker. Hugs and tears alike in every huddle.

But these sad memories were fuel for me on the walk down. Drums before a skirmish. An application of warpaint. I carried a banner I'd found in front of me: a great triangle of sequinned black and gold, our school colors. I was ready.

I could smell the Vice Principals' jawlines before I could see their office block. Every day a fresh shave, every staff meeting an attack of mid-shelf cologne. Underbites on each of them that had never been fixed. Waxed forearms with popped veins that would've made the front office staff gaga if they all hadn't been terrified of Coach's personal defense line.

"Help you, Fitz?" one of them asked. 'Russell' or something just as baritone. The blondest and newest of the trio, trained to be a junkyard dog like the other two. But we called him 'Eight' since he patrolled that grade's wing.

"Here to see Coach," I said, unfurling my flag. I presented it to Eight with purpose and meaning and lies in my heart. "It's important."

I'd beelined over to the Principals' office after chancing on a pair of randy high schoolers who'd come down on the bus from the hilltop campus. Before I turned the hose on them, I'd caught them fingering each other in front of Mrs. Trapp's Art studio, and they'd scared the Color Guard on their way out to practice. One of the girls on the squad had dropped her black and gold banner, and I'd brought it with me now like a winged herald of glad tidings.

Eight latched onto the flagpole like a new toy, and I pivoted around the cloth in an underarm turn and into the first corner of the hallway before he could recover.

It was like dancing with Jan Allen. Made me sad to think of cha chas and rhumbas and box steps we'd never finish. I thought of her girlfriend, Belinda, who would never dip her as well as I might.

Six popped out of his hovel on the left as I entered, barricading the way forward, saying, "Can't rightly say if Coach is in now, Mr. Fitz."

"Not looking for him," I said, pushing ahead. I was mustering up my best crazy eyes, like Jan Allen had made in the days before she got fed up with me and left. "It's you, Six. Just you." A feathered wedge of brunet bangs hung down over his brow, and I held him by his bricked shoulders. "You're wanted out by the bus stop. Those high schoolers are back on their frotteurism again, and I need you to be our man on it. So are you on it?"

The light changed in Six's eyes as he mumbled out "goddamnitwaithere," and then sprinted down the hallway with Eight to defend our school against the heaviest of heavy petting.

And there I was: alone now in the paneled hallway of particle-board wood and yellowing class photos, right up until Seven's door creaked open. I could hear his wood-bead bracelets clacking before he could step into the hall and block my way.

"Whatever you've got, Mr. Fitz, it can wait," Seven said. He'd spread his knotted arms in front of him and above me, a bodybuilder in a bear pose. "Coach is due up in the field house for last period. Laps today. Maybe sprints. Totally important."

Seven's hair was black as a goth kid's diary. It spiked out of the sides of his head in cartoon haystacks of pomade and determination.

"Totally," I nodded, getting in close. I made like I wanted to lambada with Seven, which gave us both certain kinds of feelings—new, important feelings—but then I rapped my knuckles on Coach's cheap particle wood door behind him at the last second.

Seven's wax-candled face tapered into a snarl the second we

both heard Coach bark out, "Door's open!"

"Don't mind me," I said, patting his deltoids. Seven growled, good dog that he was, but I couldn't stick around to give compliments. I had plans.

Sunlight streamed in through the window that looked out over the west lawn of Klaus W. Tripeltrübel middle school. Dust motes drifted in the air, making the halo effect on the man all the more pronounced.

"Color me impressed, Fitz."

In his glory, Principal Coach was a protagonist of a man, with a handlebar mustache and a close-cropped mohawk. Everything below the neck the build of an ex-college football star, trapped now in fitted khakis and a gingham tie. Wild rumors flitted down from the administration claiming he'd once QB'd for Syracuse, tore through an M.Ed. program after an injury, and then married his cheerleader girlfriend after a pregnancy scare that turned into an actual pregnancy once they put their backs into it. Their American dream was the most American of all the American dreams.

"I thought for certain I was scheduled to cover final period again, but here you are."

"Here I am," I said. "Barely. Seven almost stopped me. Good defense on that one."

Coach looked past me and into the bare hallway, empty now of VPs.

"Not good enough," he said, touching the college ring on his finger. Like his wedding ring, the jewelry burrowed into his knuckles like it was practicing autoerotic asphyxiation. I daydreamed of something gangrenous happening. "You've got three minutes to tell me what you need before I cut for the gym," he said. "Can't be late or the kids'll think they've run off another substitute."

Two weeks ago, Mr. Connolly—who taught the 'Career Explorations' class in the mornings, Phys Ed in the afternoons—had been caught high on ketamine he'd scrounged from who knows where. In his best impression of leadership, Principal Coach had driven Connolly to the local rehab and had taken over the last period of the day from the man, forcing the students to run laps since he didn't know what else to do with them if it didn't involve line formations and pass plays.

"Heaven forbid," I said. Coach's ass cheeks rested on the lip of his desk. I watched him bob up and down as he flexed and relaxed his glutes. "Now I know you're a busy man, and I won't julienne words. The union just needs you to sign off on two little things and one big thing."

Principal Coach smirked. "Bearer of bad news from the Local #1135, are you?"

"It's the job," I said. I was unflappable. "Item #1: we need a fire extinguisher next to the band room's interior doors. It's going to require a cut into the stonework if you want it to match the set." And then I shut the hell up.

First one to talk in a negotiation has lost, I remembered someone once saying. When Jan Allen told me she was leaving, I'd talked first and asked why.

"Since this isn't a fine china pattern, you go and tell Pity," Coach began, eyes closed now, "to pony out and grab a metal-and-glass box rig, punch a couple of heavy mollies into the wall, and then hang the new extinguisher up. No need to make anyone suck in aerosolized brick."

"Done," I said, surprised. Unlike Jan Allen's revelation about whom and what she loved, this was going well. "Item #2: we need $100 for the French and Geography classrooms. I could get it out of petty cash right now and have everything set up in an hour."

"Slow down there, Fitz," Coach said. "Devil's in the details. What are we talking about here?"

I puffed out my cheeks. I was ready to hoot, throw feces, make war. "A Blu-ray player for French, a new map for Geography. I could rig it up before they came back in the morning."

Our principal took his time on this one. Leaned his head back, gave pause.

"Buy the map for Mr. Grigsby. Get Pity on the installation."

Dust motes ripped around the room in whorls and waves, dancing and falling.

"And Mademoiselle Flaneur needs?" he continued.

"A Blu-ray player."

"Take the business card, but make certain the thing can play DVDs, too," he said. "Bring back the receipt or I'll turn campus into a smoke-free zone."

The very idea. I was two for two, though, so my hackles were down.

"That's fair," I said. "Ready for the big ask?"

"Shoot," Coach said, reloading his crossed arms like they were empty.

"Thursday nights," I said, ready-steady, "are henceforth optional, not mandatory."

I was expecting thunder and lightning. Something painful and loud.

Coach sniffed, "You go to hell."

So here was the firmament, the levee unbroken. The cessation of chewed gum and bouncing buttocks.

"I knew you were going to hate it," I said. "But you're a reasonable man. You know forcing the teachers and staff to show up to the night games isn't right. On top of that, it's unfair."

Our principal's posture stiffened, and I knew right then I'd lost. Our dance was over.

"Unfair?" He said it back to me. "Unfair? Well, that may be true. But what it is is contractually obligated. Page 17 in your employee handbooks, if memory serves—and it assuredly does serve—and what it is is a show of loyalty to our students. And what it is is a sacrifice. A necessary one at that."

He paused, lifted one cheek to fart, started chewing his gum again and grunted. Flatulence wafted in the air between us.

"Listen here: if I can sacrifice my afternoons to fill in because Mr. Connolly's drying out down the road," Coach continued, "then you all can sure as shit show up for an hour once a week to support the squad. You hear me?"

And then the desk bouncing started again, and so did Coach, and then the scent of the man's gases was gone. Somewhere in the room, an alarm was vibrating.

"That's time," he said, arms uncrossing now. He moved to the door and grabbed a whistle off the coat peg. "See your sweet asses in the bleachers come Thursday night."

Home was a Cape Cod the color of a fresh bruise in the middle of ivy-choked Tudors. Jan Allen and I had purchased it back in the '90s, sometime right after grunge and flannel. Our realtor was a spiteful widower, angry and bitter now that flipping property had become a younger person's game. Told us we should buy the place because it'd be a middle finger to the socialites who lived around us.

"This used to be the community gardener's home," he explained, tapping his cigar ash onto the living room carpet. "Back when this hellscape was a damn community."

Jan Allen and I made an offer on the house that same afternoon. On the day we closed, she pocketed the keys, I shaved in the bathroom sink, and we lindy-hopped until we crashed into the hearth. After an ice pack and some takeout Chinese, we rode each other on the berber carpeting until we were dehydrated. I would've thought we were happy back then. Might've just been the low interest rates.

After making nice with Coach in his departure from the office and then beelining toward my driveway, Jan Allen was there, crouched on the stoop. Next to her was the girlfriend, Belinda, who held her arm like they were conjoined. The pair of them rose from their squat when I slowed and pulled into the drive, and I saw them as they would be seen: Belinda, short and feral, ropey with muscle from working at the kennels, and Jan Allen, tall as a motherfucker, which she was now. Or she always had been.

"Jan Allen," I said. "Belinda." In the old westerns I liked to watch, cowboys greeted each other with names and nods, not pleasantries.

"Good to see you, Fitz," Jan Allen said. My surname was her pet name for me. Until a year ago, the name had been hers, too, right up until it wasn't anymore.

"Good to see you, too," I lied. We both lied. It was the same now as waving 'hello.'

There was a pause in the air as pregnant as we'd never been. Next to my ex-wife, Belinda stared me down, unblinking, the white of a sharpened canine in her snarl for me to see.

"I know I asked this last week, but is there any chance you're ready to close?" Jan Allen asked. "We won't have a buyer much longer if you keep doing this."

"No?" I said. There would be a cigarette in my hands if I could just make them leave.

"Then like I said last week: go fuck yourself," she said, gutting past me toward the rig. Belinda loped right in step with her, growling and looking tired and angry and fierce. I'd never smelled venom before, but the stink of hatred on her was something awful. "Let me know if you ever want to stop paying your half of the mortgage, you idiot."

While I still squatted at the old homestead, Jan Allen still drove our black truck, with the big payload neither of us would ever need. In the moment she and Belinda knifed past me, I watched as the girlfriend sprinted for the passenger seat, leaping up into it so she could keep hold of her hex on me, or whatever she was cooking. But Jan Allen climbed up behind the steering wheel like she was mounting a Clydesdale, and I remembered that we'd once been in love.

"I saw a bird die today," I yelled to her. It was tough to get her attention over the V12 diesel, but I pressed on. "It was there one minute, funneling pasta, and then it wasn't."

"What?" she yelled, her window down.

"And I saw two teenagers with their hands in each other's pants," I yelled back.

Jan Allen killed the engine just then, squinting at me from

behind her wraparounds. She and gun enthusiasts wore the same eye protection.

"What?" she yelled. "Goddamn it, what are you saying?"

And I missed this house, I wanted to tell her. I missed us.

"It's been a bit of a day!" I yelled back. "I've changed my mind?"

Jan Allen and Belinda murmured under the rip of the engine. I saw teeth and consolations, saw promises being made. But then the driver's side door opened, and my ex-wife led me into our old home in a perp's escort. Strong arms, my old flame.

"This better not be a trick," she said. "We've got a pot of fettuccine Alfredo waiting for us back home, goddamn it."

I thought of Jan Allen and Belinda mixing cream and parmesan cheese in a saucepan until it blended together. Of cracking pepper over hot, flaccid noodles.

"If you're serious, initial here," she said inside the door, closing papers appearing from her vest. "And sign here." Our hands touched at the knuckles. It was the most action I'd had in months. "And here."

"Are you happy?" I asked, wondering if she smelled old smoke in the house. If she did, we'd have to pay for the cleaning. "With her?"

"I will be," Jan Allen said, flipping the paper over. Our realtor's card was at the bottom of the page, his photo embossed above the name. Red polo shirt, forearms big as Belinda's. "Sign and date here."

So I did. I watched Jan Allen force all the air out of her lungs. She flipped the water faucet on and off again. Like she was checking on the condition of the place.

"Gotta say, Fitz," she said, "this feels good. Long time coming, you know?"

"I know," I said, wondering why I gave up everything I loved without a fight. "I'm sorry."

And my ex said, "What made you change your mind?"

"If I'm being honest," I told her—and I wasn't being honest—"it's work. It's Pity and the admins and the other faculty. They look up to me now. Like I'm their defense against Coach and the VPs. It's a leadership thing, babe." I watched her flinch at the old pet name. "As above, so below, you know?"

"Not really," she said, shaking her head. Her mouth hung open, and I loved her for it.

"Do you remember dancing with me?" I asked. "Like we did that first night?"

I watched Jan Allen pick up the contract and shuffle the papers together.

"We had a good thing there for a while," she told me, smiling. "But you know that's over now, right? I'm not that person anymore."

"I know," I said. Outside, Belinda was honking the horn. One beep, two. Foot revving hard onto the accelerator for effect. A wild scream of "Let's go!" sent out from the open window and into the neighborhood.

"Well, that's me," Jan Allen said, leaning toward the door. She was almost to the foyer, to the front closet that hid nothing but pipes and galoshes now. "Look, Fitz, once we close and you move out, you should start over. Maybe find someone new. Someone who likes dancing, you know?"

I used to dream of Jan Allen and I celebrating our 80th birthdays with cake and passion. We'd travel on cruise ships to Canada because that's what people our age would do. We'd die within hours of each other—maybe from a gas leak—and our surviving pets would eat our unmoving flesh because they wouldn't receive nourishment otherwise, maybe starting with our faces because that's what they loved best. We'd love them back, though, and buy them premium kibble until the end.

"I ought to," I said. "Sure I will. I'll do that."

Then Jan Allen got that look in her eye like maybe she believed me, maybe she didn't. Like everything else I'd loved in my life, I'd given this away, too. But she nodded just the same, said nothing, then hiked back to the truck. As she revved away, I watched Belinda knife an imaginary line across her neck at me. I read it more as a note of separation from her and her lover, an end to things, less so a threat of death and great pain, and then I called Principal Coach because I knew what Belinda had meant.

The boys' early practice was just finishing up as I kludged into work the next morning. I watched the football team stream down the hill after their laps, several of them puking into the grass and making yellow puddles of eggs or chewing tobacco, maybe both. Behind them, Six, Seven, and Eight rustled them down through the grass like cowboys herding cattle, and, overhead, I swore I could hear the gulls making hungry sounds and smacking their beaks in anticipation. They had the foul appetites of dogs sometimes, and I worried about the future.

"Glorious thing to see, Fitz," said Principal Coach. He wore a black and yellow polo with a chaw packet bulge in his gums. Below us, the VPs wore the same dark shirts and bulges as Coach, like myna birds in the mating season.

As above, so below, I thought.

Coach continued, "To see these young men being whittled into war engines, you know?"

I didn't. "Got a second?"

"I will," Coach said. Then to the boys: "Shower up, dress out, and if I hear about your stench from anyone in first period, we'll do burpees until you deflate. Understood?"

And then the Greek chorus of vomit-fresh voices: "Yes, Coach, sir!" Below me, adolescents rolled down the hill in waves, bile and hope on their lips, and the VPs clapped in time.

"Now what can I do for you, Fitz?" Coach asked.

I paused. Gathered courage from the ether. "I come bearing gifts," I said.

"That right?"

"You hate teaching general Phys Ed in the afternoons," I said, "the students hate taking it from you, and you're pissed you can't make them run drills like they're your second string."

"Watch your tone, Fitz." Around us, the ground was soaking up the ovals of vomit and chaw.

"But I can do it," I said. "I can take Connolly's class off your hands."

Coach laughed then, but he still rubbed his scalp with both hands as though he were honestly thinking about it.

"What would you teach?" he asked. "Because you didn't letter in a damn thing in high school."

"Dance," I said, unfazed. "Ballroom. Swing. Not so much modern or ballet, but you know I'd get their growing hearts pumping."

"But—" Coach started.

"What I don't know," I interrupted, "I can learn and then teach the basics. I've played some ball, served some volleys. I've tagged schoolchildren with dodgeballs, and I've drawn blood. But this way, with dance, maybe I'd at least give them something I'm good at."

Coach's rubbing intensified. The folds of his neck, the bristles of his mohawk, the stubble below his mustache.

"So what I get is a free period in exchange for the faculty getting out from Thursday night games?" he said. "Is that it?"

"That's the proposal, I reckon."

"You reckon."

Scalp to earlobes, earlobes back to scalp, scalp down to bridge of his nose in a slide of thick fingers.

"You'll all be there for Homecoming, though," he whispered, "and every game during the playoffs, if we ever make them again. Every single one. You hear me?"

"I hear you," I said. "We hear you."

Coach looked out over the fields then, and I followed his gaze. Gulls flew overhead and sought out trash. In my future, I saw the shakes of nicotine-free afternoons hereafter, the sweat of young frames on freshly waxed gym floors.

"For you," Mr. Grigsby said, slipping a blue Swingline into my hands. He touched my shirtsleeve, rubbed it like a St. Christopher's medal, and I watched him kowtow away.

Around us on the Tripeltrübel gym floor that Thursday, the least athletic of the eighth-graders waltzed in uneven boxes. They stumbled over shoelaces that weren't there, groped asses by mistake or on purpose, blushing either way.

Next came Mademoiselle Flaneur. "For you," she said, nestling a Toblerone into my briefcase. She bowed as she left, and I nodded my benediction. The chocolate would be gone before final bell.

"Been like this all day, has it?" asked Pity, slipping in silently. "You and the flock?"

In the far corner, a blond waif of a boy slipped and fell while spinning his partner. The girl sighed, kept dancing to the 3/4 time signature I'd piped in overhead. Another girl from the bleachers swept in to take the boy's place, to lead, but we could all tell who was twirling whom.

I nodded. "Gifts to staunch a wound after falling on a sword, I suppose."

"What'd you say to Coach?" Pity asked.

"Nothing much," I said. "Just made a trade, fair and square."

Last in line was Mrs. Trapp, her fingers smudged with pastels. Today was an advanced session of nude figure drawing, and, judging from her state of undress, she'd served as both their instructor and their model.

"I made you a little something, Fitz," she murmured, placing something in my hands. I felt the rough fabric of a cross stitch in a hoop, set in a balsam oval. "It's nothing, really, but thank you."

We watched Mrs. Trapp straighten and march through the center of the gym, head high between the whirling dervishes of tweens and teens, then out the door toward not a scheduled football game but somewhere else. A home, maybe. Hers.

Pity said quietly, "Lookit," and I did.

There, in my hands, Mrs. Trapp had laid a pattern sewn to look like our school mascot, the Tripeltrübel Troll, outlined in black and gold, its hands dripping red arterial blood and holding a person's severed and mustachioed head, possibly Coach's. I couldn't tell, really.

"Now that's damn pretty," breathed Pity.

"No, sir, it's ugly as sin," I told him. "But it's yours if you want it."

Pictures from the Coast of France

Three days after I found a high-quality photograph of my father's penis, captured on ISO 400-speed film stock, laid out over four-color spreads on pages 56 & 57 of the Swiss export, *Der Korper*, I broke up with my girlfriend and made plans to leave for France to find a swingers' party that stopped back in 1973.

"Hmm," she said. Her name was Lucie, with stress on the second syllable. "You take after him."

We were dating for almost a year at that point, but this was the end of everything between us: the dual membership to the video store, the mixed assortment of CDs in our cars, the extra tampons I kept for her in my medicine cabinet. I wouldn't allow thoughts like hers to stay in my life like toothbrushes and hair scrunchies. I had conjugative verbs to memorize.

We were in my parents' attic, sifting through wardrobe boxes for vintage clothes to sell to the local thrift stores so I could pay down her credit card, and then there was my father's footlocker, the one with the spray-painted USMC insignia and stickers from Boblingen on the sides.

"I didn't know your father was a Marine," said Lucie.

"You haven't seen the tattoo on his shoulder," I said.

Inside were his dress blues, the white cap now crumpled and yellow with time and brow sweat. There were black leather boots, tanned and peeling, a faded Red Sox cap with a frayed lip, and a bottle of amber liquid that Lucie took to her nostrils first and then her lips.

"Whiskey," she told me between sips, her brown hair the color of loose bourbon, her credit card riddled with cash advances and balance transfers. "It's smoky." And we passed the bottle back and forth until we found the magazine.

It was on the bottom of a stack of three in the locker. Looking at the first rag, the one with captions in German I couldn't translate, I cupped Lucie's bra-hidden breasts on the sides and kissed the back of her neck while we stared down at thin Aryans from the early 1970s, locked in coy poses and sly grins on grainy color spreads, all of them Robert Shaw and Ursula Andress. There were muscles and breasts and blonds and blondes, there was my father's Red Sox cap perched on the lid of footlocker, and then there was Lucie's pierced earlobe between my teeth.

"That's good whiskey," she said. When I first met her in the courtyard pool of Colonial Acres, an apartment complex where neither of us rented, she was tanning and smoking in a lounge chair, talking to a friend of mine who'd once leased a two-bedroom, second-level corner space from the properties. The friend who I went to Finance classes with lost his deposit in the exit from Colonial Acres, deciding as a result that access to the pool for years afterward was a good start in reclaiming the damages. When he introduced me to Lucie, I thought that she looked like my mother in the sunlight, both there and somewhere else behind a pair of dark, oversized glasses, and I knew at that moment I wanted the girl who stressed the second syllable in her name with a smile and a flash of teeth.

The second magazine, something Belgian with smart layouts for the time, was chocked with photographs of young men in feathered hair and brunette women with light fluff under their arms. The magazine's house photography scheme kept to a variation of low and high f-stops and natural lighting; a subject's areolae, for example, would be in focus while the buildings of the cityscapes outside the window in the scene wouldn't. Meanwhile, the spray of ejaculate on the swath of a subject's back would be just as sharp as the captured smile on her face from the side, her teeth white and her eyelids lined with black. There would always be the tiniest of moles on her face, somewhere close to the lips and tasteful.

I read the captions in French to Lucie while she parted her lips. "Marianne gemit de plaisir," I whispered. "Elle sait ou Alec est allé."

Between glasses of pinot grigio, my mother held up flash cards to my face of words in French when I was little. A girl was 'une fille'. She wore her 'cheveux' down and had white 'chaussures' on her feet. I remembered afternoons in front of the television, absorbed after the day at elementary school, watching the broadcasts of TeleFrancais from CFTO out of Ontario, its airwaves fingering Boston but just barely. Children my age from French-speaking parts of the world told me about their lives at a volume just below shouting.

"Je m'appelle Frederic," an apple-chinned boy chimed on the television. "Mon plat prefere est le gateau," he said, pointing to a triple-layered cake of dark chocolate and ganache. He licked his lips, and I licked mine from across the Great Lakes, thirsty for a glass of milk. I still translated words into French in my head that I spoke in English aloud: 'wine' became 'vin', 'thigh' became 'cuisse', 'rope' became 'corde'. I once dated an exchange student from Lyons with Algerian ancestry in high school. She had called me her 'stupid American' while my hands crept up her skirt.

"Vous etes belle," I said to her, and I meant it. The words would last longer than she would.

Here, though, in my parents' attic, Lucie's underwear was down to her sandals when we lifted the pages of *Der Korper*. "I'm getting splinters from the floorboards," she said. I rolled away from her and grabbed a quilt from my old crib that my grandmother had stitched together while I was incubating in the womb. I imagined old women at a community center, sitting around a wooden frame with pastries and weak tea in the corner of a fluorescent-lit room, talking about my mother's healthy pregnancy.

Lucie, finishing the last of the bottle, propped up on one elbow to tell me, "Your family has this clock." I flicked my tongue across her iliac crest and bit it gently while she pointed to a picture.

The clock in the photograph looked familiar, with decorated birds and a wooden Bavarian village in green and yellow. In front of the wooden dial, however, my father was crouched down on his knees, wearing a short mat of black hair and chopped sideburns. He was resting the head of his penis on a mound of pubic hair that belonged to a woman reclining in front of him.

She was smoking and dripping. She wore a black choker that matched her dark irises. The woman was not my mother.

Behind them, another couple smoked cigarettes naked in a papasan chair, smiling and bored while it rained outside the large windows. My father, however, looked happy. When the photograph was taken, he hadn't decided yet on getting the eagle, globe, and anchor tattoo of the Marine corps. He was wearing glasses like he did in his high school yearbook photos for the basketball team.

"This is my father," I said.

"Hmm," said Lucie, sliding a thumb across the rim of her underwear.

We didn't find the vintage clothes, but Lucie felt inspired anyway. She bought a bag of hash and a three-liter of table chianti on our way home. On the third day of smoking, sipping, sleeping, and not going to class to learn about home equity loans, I told Lucie I was done. I broke the bottle on the corner of her couch and watched wine soak into her throw pillows.

"I'm sorry it had to be like this," I said. "C'est fini."

"That used to be cute," she said. "The words." She wagged her pinky in the air. She looked sober. "You're not half the man your father is."

At my parents' house, my mother was talking to friends on the phone, out on the patio. She was sipping lemonade and warming herself in the daylight like a house cat, her belly warm from the sun. My father was studying the paper in the kitchen; he was hunting for codes in the personals and reading up on the newly elected aldermen.

We looked like a father and his son. Where his hair was graying, mine was still peppercorn and thick, but the part to the left was the same. We drank pineapple juice instead of OJ. He was done with pot and had smoked the last of it after meeting my mother; I was close to losing interest in it. He played basketball in high school while I swam for the varsity team. We'd both worn outfits that showed a lot of gym-built muscle then, and we'd been laid because of it.

"You have every reason to look happy here," I said, taking the magazine out of my satchel.

The cover of the magazine had a woman lit up against a backdrop of gray sky and rain. She was holding an umbrella and nothing else but a clever smile and the look of someone who was very late. *Der Korper* was written in a black calligraphic typeface in the background. Behind me, the cuckoo clock cawed out four whistle-clicks. I turned to the largest photo in the spread of my father and the woman in the choker. He was still smiling in the photograph, and so were the post-coital friends in the chair behind him.

"Tell me about her," I said.

My father seemed to stop and listen for my mother's voice. We both heard her; she was doling out a sangria recipe to whomever was on the other end of the line. Nodding, my father stared at me and said, "I'll need this back when you're done." He turned the magazine around on the counter to face him, and I imagined he was thinking back to an afternoon in Europe years ago, to a time when he was paid money by a stranger to photograph him and a woman about his young age glisten and throb.

"What was her name?" I asked.

"That's Hannelore," he said. "Hannelore Michelis. She tasted like warm cantaloupe." On the kitchen island, a pale honeydew was aging next to the brushed-steel griddle. "She was the woman I fucked before settling for your mother."

"That doesn't tell me anything," I said. "Does Mom know about this?"

My father poured himself a glass of water. "I forgot I had that thing still," he said with a stern look on his face. "And why the hell were you poking around in my footlocker? What else did you steal?"

"The whiskey's gone," I said.

He looked puzzled. "I don't know what the hell you're talking about," he said.

"Where was this taken?" I asked.

He looked down at the photograph again, dabbing his dry index finger on the lithe stomach of Hannelore circa 1973. "Istres," he said. "France. I'd gone there on R&R from Boblingen." He looked wistful and rheumy. "Now there was a place where you could get fucked up."

Outside, my mother was telling someone, "I use pomegranate juice instead of cane sugar, sweetheart. You can taste the alcohol better that way." I thought about the balance on my own credit card, about the APR and the finance charges the books for last semester's classes had brought with them. I thought about telling Lucie I might be gone abroad over summer, but then I remembered I didn't need to. And I wondered if my father had bought my mother a black choker to wear after their first few dates once he'd returned to the States, if they'd ever had friends over for dinner before I was born.

The campus International Studies office sounded surprised when I asked about their offerings for France in the summer, and if they had anything that would count toward the Business degree, but they told me about their programs anyway: a five-week session in Paris for International Relations or the four-week exchange in

Lyons to study Fashion Design. I thought briefly about a career with the State Department and added a minor that afternoon.

Two months later, I was trying my very best not to think about Lucie an hour west of Paris, when the plane began to dip toward Charles de Gaulle the morning after I left Boston. We landed, and I trudged through the crisscross of girders and platforms and open space and bi-level walkways of Terminal 1, to a shuttle that herded me to the TGV counters.

"Le TGV," a mouse-haired girl once informed me, "s'appelle Train á Grand Vitesse. Il est tres, tres rapide!" And I believed her. TeleFrancais showed a train bulleting across vineyards and rivers, from Montpellier to Avignon. Businessmen drank coffee as their bodies hurtled. A woman in a white blouse had been reading a book. She looked up at the camera for just a moment before turning away to the window. Outside, trees and stalks blurred into greens and golds.

With the dregs of my spending limit, I fingered a machine that spoke English into purchasing a round-trip ticket from Paris to Nimes, the closest stop on my way to Istres. The voice stemming out of the terminal's speakers sounded familiar to me.

"I'm hunting a woman and her choker," I told the kiosk. "She knows my father."

For breakfast, the dining car served baked toast points soaked in eggs, cream, and honey. I ate bacon and thought I saw glimpses of cows in the fields that stretched across the countryside. I sipped on dark tea and milk and thought about calling the École Centrale, to tell them I might miss the orientation lectures later that week due to illness, but that I would be there the moment I started to feel better. Fresh, expensive slices of warm cantaloupe gave the rattling plate on the table some color. I returned to my seat and waited with a hard-on after the morning meal.

"Bonjour, Hannelore," I would say. "My father was a marine. He was on vacation in 1973."

I practiced this line in English and French into the afternoon, switching between buses, watching for hints of the coastline as I metered into Istres.

"Mon pere etait un marin Americain," I chanted. "Il etait en vacances en 1973."

When I was dropped off in a stone clearing surrounded by villas and gates, I pitched up at the sky and saw fighter jets ripping across open blue lines in exercises. I was near the air base, I reasoned, but Hannelore might well have been smoking on a windowsill above me.

I thought of Lucie as I looped through winding streets of cobblestone and asked directions from raisined men and their apple-core daughters whose ribcages poked through their t-shirts in the breeze. I thought of attic floorboards and comfortable baby blankets.

"Connaissez-vous une femme s'appelle Hannelore Michelis?" I pleaded.

I asked this of everyone as I stumbled around the commune. A pair of men in tweed near the city shoreline finally gave me an answer. They pointed to the aqueduct above me, the Pont du Gard, an ancient rampart of stone sluices the Romans erected as a gift and a reminder. "La putain Michelis?" they said and smiled. "Suivre a Chemin du Levant."

So I followed it. The Chemin du Levant, I thought, was as

byzantine as the aqueduct built by Augustus. It curved like a vascular system through Istres, circulating around busy squares and spilling into roundabouts where tiny, rusting cars centrifuged. The building numbers were chipped away in some places or were gone entirely. I looked for signs of recognition from the window shot in the photographs from *Der Körper*: billowing white drapes, a blue dress shirt hanging over a banister, Hannelore's bare toes, painted pink like her lips.

I searched for names on post boxes until a local stopped next to me.

"Madame Michelis?" I asked. "S'il vous plait, ou reside-t-elle?"

Between 16 & 20 Chemin du Levant stood a single building, the address number absent save for a single nail above the door frame. The structure was newer than the others; it rippled with red bricks instead of the stucco of the bookend buildings. Metal railings webbed across the apartment verandas where people walking below could stare up at flowerpots, lounge chairs, and ashtrays. A man in his bathrobe leaned on one stoop from high above, his testicles dangling inside the silk folds while he shielded his eyes and scoured the bay.

Inside the foyer, I glanced at the post boxes and saw that apartment #4 was the top residence. I listened for voices and movements behind doors as I climbed flights: a rhythmic kick of something steady with a level bass on the floor above, muffled by the heavy ash door; a smell of lemon, garlic, and onions in a pan on the second floor where a piece of fish or a scallop was searing; the high-pitched honk of a Peugeot outside; a man on the telephone behind the door on the third floor, his voice as squeaky as the tires splashing in the street; and then silence and sunlight streaming through 17 Ave de Chine #4, the brightness caught between the hardwood and the frame of a closed door.

I tickled out the disheveled copy of *Der Korper* from my satchel and turned to Hannelore's spread. On a shining day in 1973, a photographer took snapshots of her pale skin and her young frame. She smoked cigarettes and wore through the day a black choker, a thin ribbon of cloth that accented the soft notch between her clavicles. My father was on leave from Boblingen, his legs restless from the trip on the rail lines between Germany and the southern coast of France, here in Istres to see Hannelore again at a cafe that overlooked the aqueduct. He would have had a friend stationed at the air base, someone he might have played basketball with in high school. And there would be Hannelore, smoking and reading and watching the American boy she once met in Boblingen muddle his way through caustic French phrases he'd picked up on the train. She would have laughed at him or been bored, and there would have been a party that night where a photographer friend of Hannelore's would admire the way my father bit her shoulder throughout the evening, the man searching for something to sell in the way my father left teethmarks on her neck, imprinted like wine into upholstery, like the tap-tap-tap of knuckles on the thick wood of an apartment door.

Origin Story

Once, a geneticist lost his daughter to a methadone overdose the girl received from a treatment facility, not from the heroin that was supposed to take her life after rehab. He swore revenge against the pharmaceutical company and poisoned their batches of pill-shaped precipitates they marketed and sold to the clinics. In the aftermath that shut down PallasJones Chemicals and killed off 99.97% of the patients they treated in detox, a young addict his daughter's age rose out of her bed restraints one day with the ability to rip into people's minds and, if it pleased her, stuff back in hallucinations and nightmares like so much cotton. Like the geneticist, she vowed revenge, and she would one day find him.

Once, a survivalist with access to C4 and the phone numbers of his old Army buddies planted explosives at the base of a cell tower in the nighttime. It stormed in those late hours, raining and thundering to the point where the man didn't know if the plastique would ignite, and this was when the lightning struck the metal of the tower and snuffed the man out like a candlewick. Three days later, a slate-colored cloud appeared outside his old cabin and made a sound like the snapping of fingers, and the survivalist appeared in a bright flash, just like that, eager to learn about himself, his new powers, and the corporate office cross streets of the major telecoms.

Once, a biomedical physicist brought his work home with him. The lead shields at the R&D labs had been damaged during shipping, and beta radiation zipped through the lining as the physicist tested a new PET scan configuration. The decay participles coursed through his abdomen and pelvis, and they splattered through his DNA like paintballs and BBs, denting the alpha helices in their trajectory. Elated with her husband's joy over the successful tests, the physicist's wife made love to him, took his seed, and fused it with her egg into a zygote that grew restless and split into two embryos. While the boys kicked their mother in the womb, their father's newfound cancer killed him quickly, blooming up from his testes into his kidneys, his pancreas, his lungs. Later, the twins never could remember their father, but they remembered well their mother's tears. In puberty, when all things changed, one of the boys would know, as well, what it was like to run very, very fast, and the other would know how to solve math and logic problems with a synaptic velocity that outmatched his brother's.

Once, I overheard you with your friends. At the birthday sleepover, when they asked you what I did for a living, you told them I was a superhero. Not a media coordinator, like my work badge says, but a superhero. While you and your friends slept with your blankets kicked off that night, I took stock of the garage and found rope and a gardening claw that could be kludged into a grappling hook. I grabbed a roll of electrical tape that could be used for handcuffs if the Army surplus store didn't carry any. I looked online for krav maga class schedules and saw that the Tuesday night sessions would be fine while the Thursday nights would have to be worked out somehow with your father's business dinners. I ordered an *Acrobatics for Adults* DVD series. I took a good look into the kitchen and saw the dishes, the near-empty bottle of syrah on the counter, and the space between the doorframe that could hold a chin-up bar. I would learn to fight crime for you, my darling, but first I would learn pressure points and knife defense techniques.

Replay

From a second-story walkup at the Sandringham Flats, a man jumps out a window and splashes glass down onto the pavement of Covent Gardens as his body drops and rolls into a run. Midmorning browsers at the bookstore below and old men coming out of the Ladbrokes across the street look first to the sound of the glass and then up to the shouting, and then to the small man sprinting away.

Tucked away where the runner can't see them, speakers in the street shoot out a rhythm of kettle drums and violins and cymbals, a soundtrack for the man to speed down Charing Cross Road, and he's appreciative of the noise that covers his tread. Despite the two men chasing him, who are right now this very second coming out the downstairs exit onto the lane, the runner—a man called only 'Zhou,' his family's surname—is in a good mood. He's on his way to meet up again with his contact here in England, a scientist and physician calling himself 'Saint John,' who has a penchant for strawberry ice cream and swearing in Mandarin, and he's been told he's saving the world.

But then Zhou hears the trance of the music from the speakers fall suddenly into a break, an immediate swing down into a droning, discordant chord of E and G#, as his feet fall out from below him. He stumbles, hits his head on the pavement, and, as the world snuffs out like a candle and goes black, he wonders if he's actually heard the gun go off from behind him, or if the pain in his spine might have come from something other than a bullet.

The operative, a Chinese national named 'Zhou,' leaps out of and dashes as fast as he can away from the men in a second-story apartment this morning. He's done this before, he knows this, the act of hitting a hard surface and rolling with the momentum; he remembers capturing a Kowloon gangster back home once using this same technique in a police pursuit back in Shanghai. But right now, Zhou knows the men above him have pistols dangling from their underarms, in holsters meant to be discreet, and the bulges in the fabric are there just the same, and so he zigzags down Charing Cross Road, finding cover where he can.

His handler, an old physician named Saint John—"It's pronounced 'Sin Jin,' actually," he's told Zhou—had instructed him to go to this flat under the pretense that he would be there to purchase an assault rifle. Illegal to own in England, the rifle would be sold by a small-arms dealer who also had in his inadvertent possession, up until just a few moments ago, a small chrome box that the governments of China and England, respectively, would prefer not be sold to private citizens. And while neither country could afford to pay what the dealer wanted for the box out of public funds, they could and did provide a work visa for a Chinese officer who was familiar with the dealer's suppliers, and they could also deposit cash into the checking account of Saint John, a former MI5 staff physician who retired to Shanghai years ago and who now performed attaché work when the money was right.

"Cut him off!" one of the men yells.

To save himself some minutes on the way to the tube station, where he must be in order to meet Saint John on time, Zhou strafes through a busy roundabout that stands between him and Leicester Square. From somewhere around him in the circle, kettle drums and cymbals and a string section play over the twinkling of a rondo he remembers.

"Don't lose him!" the other man says, leaving the chase, and the man's partner continues his pursuit.

Between the waves of the vehicles around him, Zhou thinks back to his conversations with the good doctor, to the histories they've shared with each other. He'd told Saint John about his far-away move from western China out to Shanghai, about his time on the police force, about how London reminds him just a bit of his adopted city.

"It's the same for me," the doctor had said, licking at his ice cream. "I suspect that's why I retired there. Reminded me just enough of London."

As he runs, Zhou thinks back to the great red and blue and yellow-white signs stippling out around Shanghai's endless streets, to the rivers of concrete and to its traffic patterns, so much of it here like it is back there, congested and relentless with movement.

Now, outside Leicester Square, Zhou rests for a moment at the interior circle of the roundabout, and he watches one of the men with guns from next to the great concrete column, while Fiats and Peugeots and BMWs honk at him. He is causing himself undue notice in public, he realizes, and then this is when he recognizes the driver of a black lorry, just before it jumps the curb and pulls him under its front bumper. Through the crushing sound of bone around his brain, through the pain and shock of the impact, Zhou can hear the music fade out alongside him.

Zhou's vault down from a broken window and the subsequent run from his pursuers this morning feels familiar, like he's done it all before, all the polygons of the Covent Garden neighborhood and adverts just bland swatches of color, none of it new, nothing to make a landmark out of should he need to find his way through the alleys and side roads. He stamps hard against the pavement and manholes and spray-painted bits of concrete as he runs and splashes through small, clear puddles on the road. In full linen suit, tie, vest, and Spanish leather shoes, he imagines he might look a bit odd to those he stripes by on the sidewalk, but he runs with purpose. He runs for three important reasons: (1) because he must make it to the Leicester Square station by noon exactly; (2) because Doctor Saint John requires the small chrome box Zhou is carrying; and (3) because there are two large, sprinting men chasing after him.

Reason #1 is the most immediate. The London Underground system is both renowned and notorious for its efficiency and its tempered-steel precision, unlike the rails of his native Shanghai's Metro. The tube fills and empties stations with unparalleled exactness. It assures passage, it instills punctuality in the minds of millions, domestic and abroad, and it symbolizes the English character, or so Saint John's told him. It is, above all else, proper and accountable. According to the city clock that Zhou is right at this very moment passing under, it is 11:52am. He decides he will circumvent the roundabout and make his way down the flight of the escalator by taking steps two at a time, and he will remember that it is "stand on the right, walk on the left" with regards to the ramped mass of the queue. Above him, from speakers he can't see, a heavy rondo of drums and strings pipes out and matches his pace.

Reason #3 is the least immediate. Zhou is naturally faster than the two men chasing him, but the heels of the leather shoes slow him down, albeit slightly, to the point where his and his pursuers' respective paces are about the same. The men chasing him wear track suits and trainers; Zhou wears a tailored three-button with a silk tie made into a four-in-hand knot. Another factor as to why Reason #3 is the least immediate is the fact that, should the men actually catch up with Zhou for the purpose of retrieving the small package he's stolen—'retrieved' is the word Saint John used—Zhou will use his knowledge of kung fu to physically impair if not outright disable or kill his attackers.

Should this contingency occur, it'll be best if Zhou makes use of a hiding place from which to surprise the two men chasing him. He's almost certain they are both carrying firearms, and so a hiding place from which to crush their tracheae will be most advantageous. From his vantage point on the street, it is a comfort to know that so many corners and obstructions are available to him.

It is 11:53. Zhou zooms down the cobblestone like a zephyr, patting his left breast pocket every so often to ensure that the small package is still safe within the silk lining of his blazer. He can feel the chrome exterior of the miniature box he carries, five centimeters by three centimeters by a final centimeter. It flounces in his pocket, so he straightens his jacket as he runs to keep the interior bouncing to a minimum.

And while Reason #2 is neither the most nor the least immediate, it is assuredly the most important. The good doctor requires the contents of the package Zhou now couriers for him. Its contents are precious; its potential effects are reviled. *So small yet so absolutely horrible*, is what the Englishman has told him. Under the bars of the rondo, Zhou imagines Saint John sitting now at an open table, licking ice cream he's purchased from a vendor at South Kensington Station, where Zhou will hopefully connect to him if he is on time at Leicester Square.

A minute later, Zhou glimpses the great green park that is centered in the Square a little off in front of him. His lungs burn past the currency exchange, a dry cleaner's, and the small café where he had breakfast earlier this morning. The rondo speeds up as Zhou increases his own velocity, as he flits towards the entrance of the Odeon movie theater, a place where film premieres are held when the stars, starlets, and directors of Hollywood and London come to unveil their latest works to the United Kingdom. *There must have been a premiere last night*, Zhou reasons as he watches local journeymen disassembling a line of steel-girded barriers. As he reaches the pipe linings, he leaps with one supple-leathered shoe in front, one shoe kicked back and behind him, and he lands on cobblestone in a hurdler's wave, leaping over the spots where a red carpeted trail flowed only hours ago.

It is 11:55. The two men chasing Zhou are indeed carrying fire-arms. The weapons are hidden in plastic and nylon strappings that fit snugly under their arms and across their backs. They, like Zhou, keep their jackets close to their bodies by pulling down on them toward their pants as they run. As they approach the steel line of barriers, the assailants also jump over them, but their stunted leaps slow them down. They do not have the physical capabilities that

Zhou possesses, movements that allow him to retain momentum and balance. These men carrying small but powerful Astra .45s do not comprehend the body's center of gravity. Meanwhile, Zhou speeds ahead with purpose.

Seconds past the girders, he turns left down a slight side street, past the sign of the red circle and the blue crossing bar that reads "Leicester Square." In the park are mothers with small children, old men in wool caps who smoke pipes, businesswomen on lunch break. They look up from their books and their phones and their newspapers to see Zhou running past them in his full suit, tie, vest, and incredibly nice shoes. The shoes are part of the foreign costume Saint John has provided for his agent.

In his native China, in the Hotan oasis of the desert, where his extended family lives, Zhou normally wears clothes similar to those on the men who are chasing him, at least when he is not on assignment. He is one of the Republic's region-free policemen, sent across borders like a ranger. But London is so very far from home, and the volume of the rondo he's heard so many times since coming to the city reminds him of this.

Before meeting with the employer of the two men chasing him this morning, Zhou was told by Saint John to wear the tailored suit he provided. "It'll cause less suspicion," the physician explained. "Make you look more like a proper villain, like someone who needs a weapon in this town."

Zhou recalls his meeting with the sweaty arms dealer just minutes ago. At the lush penthouse flat of the villain with potential gout, Zhou brought with him a large briefcase made of tanned alligator skin and gilded handles and polished fittings. The large man's two associates—the men who are currently chasing Zhou—

patted the undercover policeman down, turning him roughly around and between the two of them. They required Zhou to reveal the contents of his briefcase first. Zhou knew they would, and he proceeded to carefully open the latches and the briefcase's lid. Inside were more pound sterling notes than any of the men in the room had ever seen at once in their entire lives, the fat man included. Doctor Saint John had insisted that a small plastic bag of cocaine accompany the stacks of bills.

"As a personal touch," the Englishman had replied. "Something a scoundrel would throw in as a gift."

The most disagreeable dealer then removed the small chrome box that the physician had warned Zhou about the evening prior. Greedily, before Zhou could touch the box with his thin hands, the villain had grasped the briefcase, pocketed the plastic bag, and then snapped his fingers. Two Astra .45s had appeared, just as Zhou suspected they might. With a quick kick to the left henchman's heel and a gouge to the right man's sternum, Zhou had given himself enough time to surprise the fat man with a knee to the back of the spine.

Time seemed to pull apart more slowly then, like cold honey, like he was no longer watching these dangerous events through his own eyes but through the lens of a camera. Every detail captured as though in a photograph, Zhou watched the package of extreme importance flip up into the air in whirls. Using the arms dealer's left shoulder as a ledge, the young agent from China leapt up into the air to catch the precious box. For Zhou, then, the rest was a blur of repeated kicks, slammings of doors, and tight corners as he made his way to the second-story window and then to the street below with the package in hand, down to where a staccato set of kettle drums played over a sonata on repeat.

The small chrome box, though, now flops in Zhou's left breast pocket. He pats the space over his heart again, making certain the package is secure and safe. Entering the pit of the station, Zhou leaps down steps towards the turnstiles, feeling in his watch pocket for his day pass. He runs, yes, but Zhou takes time to slide through the scanner; he doesn't want to force attention on himself in close quarters. The mass of people is dense here, and it'll get thicker as he descends to the line.

It is 11:57. The people in the park might not think much of Zhou's hurried run past their favorite lunch spots, but they might also think more about him when they see two men running together toward Zhou's last-seen direction. They imagine Zhou to be a terrorist, a foreign-born criminal at the very least, and that these two men are authorities who are pursuing him for committing a crime. But these lunching individuals are uncertain; typically, on the television, it is the well-dressed individuals who are innocent, and the shabby looking ones who have committed crimes. The two men chase while they sweat in their track suits, both of them dressed for but not used to this kind of endurance.

Across London, the good doctor checks his watch. He imagines that Zhou is now racing toward the Leicester Square platform, breathlessly making his way down the tunnels to board the tube with his small package in tow. He imagines a variation on the complications Zhou is currently experiencing, but he doesn't allow for the possibility that Zhou's two pursuers have just now seen him dash around the white tiles of the station below.

—

Zhou sees these situations forming, though, and he spies the two men from the corners of his eyes, now tromping down the long flight of movable steps quickly. He is at the bottom of the escalator, having descended from several stories above him down on steps made of great metal teeth. And while the train has not arrived, not yet, it will soon, but it will also stall for a few moments to ensure that its boarding passengers do not have any limbs protruding from its sliding doors. *Mind the gap*, a voiceover chimes. *Mind the gap*. But because the train is not here, Zhou must stop and prevent the men from following him. He must fight.

It is 11:58, and Zhou now crouches close to the tiled wall that juts out from the escalators. He is poised here, ready to leap, ready to crush tracheae if required. He hopes to avoid this action because it will cause delays. But Zhou cannot be delayed, and Saint John absolutely will not be delayed. The doctor will continue to eat his ice cream, and he will take it with him the moment the train shows up and Zhou is or is not onboard. In either case, Zhou imagines, Saint John will walk quickly to an exit, and he will hail a car to take him to Heathrow for the scheduled flight. Zhou must make it to South Kensington on time.

So Zhou's left foot spins hard into the first man's upper chest the moment the man's face files past the tiled corner. The force of the blast takes his breath from him, and the man stumbles back into his partner. Zhou acts quickly, turning the corner to confront his pursuers, kicking now at the same man's right hand, the one with the drawn Astra. The gun spins and flies down onto the platform concrete, and Zhou lands a roundhouse into the first man's forehead. Again, the egregiously expensive leather of Zhou's shoe connects to the man's skin and bone, and motion and energy are transferred from the beam of Zhou's foot to his sock to his shoe, and then to the broad bone of the man's skull. He is propelled back into his partner's gut, and the first man is hammered into unconsciousness. His partner, however, is not severely damaged, nor is he without his weapon as he grips furiously up from his seat on the steps.

A crowd of people pools at the bottom of the escalator, but Zhou cannot delay; he hears the noon train approaching, coming into the station now. He can feel the tube's wind on his face before he can see the train itself. But there is the matter of the second man with the weapon to deal with first. Deftly, deftly and quickly, Zhou rolls forward—he rolls below the man's line of sight—and gets his jacket, his vest, his tie, and his pressed pants filthy with the black soot for which London is famous. When his tumble deposits him directly in front of the second man, his clenched fists find the hem of his opponent's jacket, and so Zhou pulls hard. The second man, the man with the drawn weapon, is yanked down onto the hard tiling, his jaw connecting with faux ceramic, and the force of the blow causes the man to spurt out a stream of blood onto the pool of people to his left. The man trips, falls, and collapses near the descending steps of the escalator. Zhou turns and flits quickly toward the open doors. A woman screams.

It is 11:59am. Saint John, still licking his strawberry melba, looks to his watch, looks toward the tunnel, but he remembers it's early. The lunch crowd at the station queues up for their meetings somewhere else. He sees a woman in a blue mackintosh with gray piping, looking down the tunnel toward the direction he knows

Zhou's train will shoot out from, and he imagines the operative's car hushing and chugging onto the platform at Leicester Square. He envisions the net exchange of people from the interiors of the car to the concrete and vice versa. Those getting onto the coach, including Zhou, are hurrying toward their destinations, their own packages in tow. Here, at South Kensington, the woman in the blue mack checks her watch as Saint John again checks his own.

So much depends on a minute, he thinks, rising from his seat.

Travelers race from the unconscious man and his bleeding associate. Passengers getting off the train and onto the platform hurry quickly away from the mess of splotched red while Zhou peers out through the glass of the car as he boards. He watches his opponent slowly stand up from the ground with frustration and impatience, and then the doors close, something hisses, and slow movements can be seen as the Leicester Square station pulls back from the young operative's sight. Zhou feels for the metal and plastic box in his breast pocket; it is still there, and he relaxes just slightly in the car's trembling.

At the lip of Leicester Square, there is a pause in the movement of the car, a hiccup in the procession of the train's pull, a voice-over—"Mind the gap"—and then all is normal again. *The train has allowed another passenger on*, he thinks. *Maybe more.*

Five stops away, the Englishman looks up at the terminal to see that the tube from the Square is on time. He licks again and again at his strawberry melba cone as he imagines the path of the line: Leicester to Piccadilly, Piccadilly to Green Park to Hyde, Hyde to Knightsbridge, and then the young officer will arrive, package in tow. Saint John checks his watch once more and doubts very much that they will have time to pick up Zhou any ice cream before they leave together for Heathrow.

It is 12:15. The doctor remembers from the old days with MI5 that the wait for the handoff is the most difficult part of the operation. For the sake of mankind, however, a healthy, industrious, Chinese operative must absolutely be on his way here. The end of the world, he thinks, is difficult to wait out. The minutes count down: 12:01 at Leicester Square; 12:04 at Piccadilly, still good; 12:07 at Green Park, also good; Hyde Park at 12:11—the wait is causing Saint John's pate to shine and sweat, but the ice cream is still cold in his hands—Knightsbridge at 12:15. In approximately two minutes, if the London Underground is worth a damn in sterling, an athletic Chinese agent with a solid appetite for fried fish should step off the train with a chrome box on his person. The physician begins to nibble on the edges of his waffle cone.

And when the 12:17 line from Leicester Square pulls into the platform, Doctor Saint John begins to respire normally until he sees the broken window on the third car. When the doors hiss open, the physician hears the shouts and yells and screams of dozens of passengers; they escape quickly from a man at the back of the car. The man in the Adidas sports jacket with an Astra .45 crouches over a bloodied figure on the floor of the train, the body's face visible from one of the rear doors. The man in the sports jacket's pale mouth is crusted with blood, but his maw is scrunched into a grin as he removes something from the still form's well-fitting vest.

It is a small box, Saint John knows; it is chrome and contains something that is valuable beyond the man holding the gun's knowledge. And as the shooter stands up, the doctor sees the end of the world step off the platform and head towards the city streets of London in a violating daze. Meanwhile, a bulleted Chinese policeman lies still at the bottom of the train from Leicester Square. Blood pools and collects on the linoleum floor below him.

With a faint shrug in his shoulders and a tremor in his heart, Saint John steps quickly for the street exit from the station. Police vans and cars assemble and blare their sirens, but the queue for taxis nonetheless fills and empties, and the doctor is next in line.

Instead of meeting a team of scientists near MI5, he will circumvent them and travel to Heathrow early. He will wait and board the afternoon flight bound for Shanghai, but the seat next to him will be empty. Still, the Englishman will fly to mainland China. He will ride in his fast automobile currently sitting at the airport to his summer home. He will pay his house sitter handsomely, more than what they've agreed upon beforehand, he will gaze longingly at her soft buttocks as she walks down the drive, and he will kiss his debilitated wife on her forehead and tell her that something went wrong. Something that was never meant to happen will assuredly occur now because of a simple error in time. He will read to his wife from an English translation of the Brothers Grimms' collected works, as she trembles in her chair from early Parkinson's. On her best days, he remembers, she will smile at the parts when the hero beats the devil in competition.

But now, as Saint John steps from third to second in line at the curb, for some unknown reason, he can hear music play above the din of the sirens and cars. The ice cream cone in his hand starts to taste a bit metallic, a bit off, a bit like the rusting scoop with which the little coquette at the counter used to yank this filth out of its cardboard tub. So the physician tosses his ice cream in a rubbish bin just a few paces away, knowing that nothing will ever taste like strawberry melba again. The music above him swells from a fast-paced rondo into a low-key chord of sound, an E and a G# played together in stark discord, but it is time to go now, and there is a plane to catch at Heathrow.

Musn't be late, he thinks.

Embryology

There was Charles Goodyear, who first stumbled onto the process of vulcanization by dropping sulfur-infused rubber on a hot stove. There was Alexander Fleming, who discovered penicillin after he left his bacteria plates open to spores while he went on vacation. And then there was Vicki Clive, who made a Gummi Bear dance only after her sister called in late December to tell her that she was a billowing eight weeks' pregnant. Victoria—'Vicki' to her sister, her parents, her longer-term boyfriends—had seen twitches in the bend of the gelatin and the carnauba wax bears in her university lab, but at first there hadn't been so much life instilled in the candy as there had been the slow kick of neurons between citrus-flavored axons and dendrites. She wanted and waited for their little corn-syrup mouths to speak, and the ones she felt move, even slightly, she froze in the Cell & Molecular Biology department's ample supply of liquid nitrogen. The ones that were left in the wholesale bags she ate; she needed the sugar late at night. Vicki consumed dozens of contingent little vessels for life, sucked them down to build energy in herself so that she could attempt to make their mouths move on their own, whether it was to sing or scream.

And, ultimately, there was Kevin, the moving and dancing candy bear, but first there was the lab phone to answer.

"It's already a fetus, you know?" said Elizabeth, her sister, squeaking over the phone and speaking of her own growing experiment.

"Since the start of your ninth week, yes," Vicki told her. "That's the gestation cutoff in humans."

"Mom's thrilled, of course. It'll be weeks before the next ultrasound, but she's already purchased us a Diaper Genie."

Vicki murmured on the other end of the line, below the quiet, shining fluorescents within the university. "That's the contraption that twists the dirty diapers into a cone," she said.

"And Dad's asked for a copy of the ultrasound photos. Isn't that sweet?" asked Liz. "Mom has started calling him 'grandpa' already." And Elizabeth would giggle; at 26, she still giggled like she did in the room they once shared.

"Where will you keep it?" Vicki asked. "The Diaper Genie, I mean. Won't it smell?"

This was where the conversations would usually end, with Vicki in the university lab, in among the NMR spectrometers and PCR banks, and with Elizabeth thinking of the future. Elizabeth's husband, Hal, would call her from the kitchen to inquire about whether or not she could eat onions while pregnant, or mussels, or linguine with basil. Elizabeth would say her goodbyes, and Vicki would put down the lab phone and make coffee. She would tap the glass of the agar tubes in which little red, green, and orange bears floated in colloid solutions. She would whisper to them while ground beans percolated in the corner, would worry in the meantime if Elizabeth would call again the next day, giddy and breathless and growing.

—

Born three years after her sister, little Victoria had burned the family's Persian on top of a heated Weber grill the same year Elizabeth was finishing Kindergarten. It was cold outside, she told her parents, and the cat looked chilly and hungry right before the family's dinner of roasted corn and ribs, so she dropped it onto the still-hot metal of the grill once she could pull the patio chair close enough. The burns were bad enough that the family had taken the cat to the vet for euthanasia, and then they buried it in the front yard instead of the back, calling it an accident despite the best of intentions. While her sister read the entire Nancy Drew series between the ages of nine and twelve, Vicki skipped the better portion of first grade for more advanced classes without nap time mats and warm cinnamon rolls served with milk. She learned about decimal remainders and long division while boys her same age, the ones who pulled at her pigtails, learned about the vast complexities of multiplying single digits. As Elizabeth began to realize the superiority of OB's bullet-shaped and applicator-less tampons, the budding Vicki was knee-deep in nitrate studies and the verdant soil in which her tomato vines grew with fervor. When Elizabeth left her undergrad days at Boston College with a bachelor's in Sociology and a vicious case of trichomoniasis, her younger sibling was a year ahead of her at MIT, finishing her Master's in Cell & Molecular Biology, a dual bachelor's in Microbiology and Biochemistry under her belt already, all tassels and medals and suma cum laude.

"The burning and itching is normal," said Vicki that graduation weekend. "Ask the health center physician for Metronidazole while you've still got the cheap insurance."

"Are you driving home this weekend?" Elizabeth asked. "I'm making Cherries Jubilee."

"I can't," Vicki muttered from a well-funded tower on the edge of campus. "I've got an interview in Baltimore." There was a pause and some shuffling in the background. "Oh, and the discharge from the bacteria you caught can be pretty potent. It can eat a hole in cotton underwear," Vicki offered, thinking of the men who had come to her sister's dorm rooms and apartments over the four years she'd spent at school.

Back in October, when Elizabeth told her sister that she and her husband were trying to conceive, Vicki got drunk that same night on blue curaçao and purchased the bag of Gummi Bears, less for the purpose of making new life and more for the sugar rush. On the phone the next morning, when Elizabeth mentioned that she felt hungrier and more sexually rambunctious since she had stopped taking Ortho-Tricyclen, Vicki, still inebriated from the night before, pulled out her thick manuals and her passwords to PubMed to search for information on the totipotency of stem cells. Her mind and heart felt as primed as her sister's womb.

And on New Year's, after enough time had passed to call it a sure thing, Elizabeth and her husband celebrated a bubbling collection of cells not by sipping champagne, but by toasting each other's virility with sparkling white grape juice. Elizabeth called to tell her sister about the white stick with the plus sign she had urinated on that very morning, and Vicki, her teeth beheading another artificially colored animal near the chilly waters of the Charles River, mixed drinks again from the laboratory's hidden collection of almost-empty bottles.

In mid-January, many days and bottles of blue curaçao later, there was the flicker of a head jiggle from GB019, the mylar-bag brother of eighteen stoic, little bears before him. Vicki remembered that she had treated herself to pizza afterwards. She wondered, though, and just for a moment, what kind of alleles the delivery boy had been carrying around in his scrotum, if he would ever consider throwing a frisbee with or hosting a tea party for a Kindergartener to be essential bonding activities, if he would steal the high thread-count sheets from her side of the bed on cold evenings. His name tag read 'Kevin,' and Vicki believed the name was noble enough for her own sweet and chewy child, were she to conceive.

"How old was your maternal grandfather when he died?" she'd asked, inviting the grinning junior in to share the sliced sections of his labor—pepperoni, mozzarella, banana peppers—feeling for muscle at the shoulders of his red-and-white checked shirt. "Do you know if he suffered from coronary heart disease?"

In the cold weeks of that winter, while restocking her supplies of gelatin, paper clips, and soy milk, Vicki encountered Elizabeth's husband at a Whole Foods near Beacon Hill. She found Hal perched next to the deep rows of pureed baby food, the sleeve of his sport coat brushing up against the small glass tubs of pulverized peas & ham.

"Hey, Vic," he ejected, grunting for some reason in his search. "Do you see the carrots here? I can't find the goddamn carrots."

Clutching the bag of candy in her hands, Victoria Clive began to rationalize how her sister could have agreed to marry Hal, could have engaged in heavy petting with him. Whether he looked like a hominid or not, the man certainly did have sex appeal: a widow's peak that touched his ghost of a sagittal crest, trapezius muscles that gave rise to a mountainous neck, hulking hands that could carry so many sacks of groceries.

They discussed Elizabeth and baby formula in the express line.

"Wait," Vicki asked. "Why are you buying baby food?"

"Liz wants us to sample them. I had to drive over for a client lunch." He looked down at the bag in her hands. "Do these things have expiration dates?" He held aloft a glass cylinder of whipped beets.

One of his great hands cradled a can of soda and a small bag of peanuts; the other splayed out to reveal five servings of Gerber in a variety of colors. Vicki's eyes flitted from the orange glow of the mango puree to the deep purple of the roasted beets.

"Yeah, so like I said, Liz wants to taste them," said Hal, not waiting for Vicki to look back up at him. "She wants to know if we should buy a food processor and make the stuff ourselves." He paused, sniffed at the man in front of them in line.

"I shave my body hair away regularly," he added, spilling this to her as though she were a different, later model of his wife. "I ask the guy at the liquor store now a lot about erotic, non-alcoholic wines. I buy a lot of candles to set the mood, you know? Second trimester?" Vicki watched Hal's eyes slip down from her face to her chest. "I've brought home literature on the Reverse Cowgirl position and how it will affect our kid's reading habits. I spend a lot of time alone in the bathroom." The cashier began to bag items from Hal's basket. "Do you know she's been talking with your mom about all this?"

"Mom didn't mention anything." She watched Hal slide a credit card out of his wallet. "Really? Reverse Cowgirl?"

"Tell me about it," said Hal, pausing here, looking now directly back into Vicki's pooled eyes. "Did you know they make lubricants that heat up when exposed to skin? You're smart; care to tell me what's the chemistry there?"

The lab freezers were filled with histology samples of so many mice, so many catalogued lots of small white rodents and their chunked-up vascular systems, their tiny hearts, their skin cells and their brains. These were the departmental favorites: the brains and the bits of the nervous system the grad students had been forced to scrape out and save in deep freeze. Slides of frontal cortex cross-sections, intact medullae, stem cells from the top of spinal columns, bits of what looked like either a period from a page of notes or the most miniscule hippocampi: they were all there and could be found in the metal boxes of the oversized fridge.

And so this was where Vicki spent the night after receiving Elizabeth's first phone call, the one where she learned her sister was pregnant. That cold January, she bent over the lip of the freezer and found the cast-offs of her colleagues' research: the bits and pieces of what might be useful later, what shouldn't go to waste after they had spent so long getting the Institutional Review Board to approve the informative deaths of so many mice.

"Never science while you're drunk," she told herself, prepping the tiny patches of smooth muscle cells and bone and brain in between sips from the blue bottle, a bag of Gummi Bears next to her on the desk. "Never, never, never."

Later, Vicki reclaimed her experiment from the incubator and safely concluded that, despite failure, both the packaging center of Jools Confectionary, Inc. and the surface of her own latex-gloved hands were relatively clean. No musculoskeletal systems had grown, no nervous systems, and, simultaneously, there was no mutant, mobile Gummi Bear strolling about her work table.

Research grants were given for conclusions less than this, she told herself, and then that was the end of 'GB001,' the first of many victims. She packed up his sugary body and dropped it into a small tub of formalin, preserving him in her purse and waiting until she could leave for home for a proper burial. Before then, she read on the bag, was the little candy figurine's obituary: corn syrup, sugar, gelatin, citric acid, yellow 5, blue 1, red 40, carnauba wax, natural and artificial flavors.

Run spectroscopy on 'natural and artificial flavors,' she told herself.

Between the final touches on her thesis, typed up during the day when she was expected to put in face time in front of her colleagues and the rest of the faculty, there were the other failures, the ones that happened sometime in the night when she was there and ready for them. There was the new approach with GB002, who was stabbed with a load of *E. coli* and was left to float in its own broth. The orangey crash dummy became infested by the end of the first day in its humid environment. There was GB003, as well, a victim of similar circumstances, drowning in a moss of *S. aureus*. GB004 was split open by the sores the *C. botulinum* colonies produced on its wee person, as was GB005 by the friendly *L. acidophilus* beasties.

Vicki failed and then dreamed these nights of hulking quadriceps, of sinewy forearms tufted with hair that held aloft bottles of baby food.

Over a lukewarm cup of tea and bourbon one afternoon, she reasoned on paper that candy originally produced in a hot oven might play a rather nice host to some hefty heat-resistant microbes. GB006 imploded from the spreading force of *S. thermophilus*; its sugary brother, GB007, was reduced to a greenish gel by its own swarm of bacteria.

The department has asked me about my extraction techniques on the S. thermophilus collections, wrote the scientist. I have concluded that absolutely no one looks at the requisition forms.

Is Hal circumcised? she penciled.

But Elizabeth would call her sister in these late winter and early spring days, complaining of her vicious need for pickles, watermelon, and funnel cakes.

"It's called 'pica'," Vicki said. "Are you taking those iron supplements your doctor prescribed?"

"They make me constipated," the booming Elizabeth replied. "I had to take a laxative that made my intestines punch up. I kept farting." And there was a pause between the loud bursts. Vicki imagined her brother-in-law's pinched face. "I've never really enjoyed pork chops, but now I can't get enough of them," the mother-to-be relayed. "Remind me: you ate paste in grade school, right?"

While cells cleaved within Elizabeth's womb, the younger Victoria would drift off at night to thoughts of plasmid replication, of microscopic bacteria dividing and growing exponentially. Entire populations, she imagined, were born and were killed in a single day. She began to wonder if maybe a viral strain would be more effective in making the Gummi Bears dance. She dreamed of electric stimulation, of stem cells and those histology samples she'd stolen when she was alone in the labs each night. She questioned if she should work her way up from Gummi Worms first (simple cell structure, asexual reproduction) before she attempted to understand the mechanics of gelatinous mammals. Vicki began on these mornings to pat her own tummy while standing in front of the bedroom mirror. At nights, she rubbed herself to sleep with two fingers, rocking her legs above her hips afterward because it seemed like the right thing to do.

"Marbles fall out of my belly button these days," Elizabeth explained. "I'm not all that poochy or anything, but—."

"Marbles?" Vicki asked. Sleep came every few days this semester.

"We're thinking of keeping the umbilical cord afterwards," Elizabeth mumbled. She was chewing something. "Out of sheer curiosity, how do you preserve it?"

Vicki pondered the mysteries of artificial and natural flavors. The Charles flowed outside her window. Snow collected on its bridges.

"Or at least some of the placenta," Elizabeth concluded. "Vicki?"

As Vicki watched for the budding of blastocysts in the candy, or what she hoped were blastocysts, she would leave the lab only for cold sushi take-out and to search for gifts for the fetus in her sister's womb. She sent soft crib blankets and thick washcloths in the mail because the drive up I-93 took more time than she was willing to donate. She boxed and shipped off plush frogs and rabbits that were light like fur in her hands. She called and critiqued suggestions for names.

"I'm not such a fan of Lionel," she said.

"Frederick?" Elizabeth asked. "Marilyn? Pauline? Dwight?"

These received hems and haws.

"Francis?" proffered her sister. "Francis would work as a boy's or a girl's name."

In her laboratory, when Vicki was not pondering names and possible facial shapes of her niece or nephew, her heart pulsed back and forth as she watched the impossible occur. The broth of a functional organism produced in GB014 made, to Vicki's delight and horror, a repetition of torso shifts in the agar tube as she sat at her station late at night. The Gummi Bear would bend against the weight of the gel around it. The plump and sugary body would jerk to the left each time it moved, a small locomotion that never got him closer to a view of the lab's third-story window. She sat and watched him like onlookers gaze at natural phenomena: sunrises, storms, Mount Aetna burning.

"Can you see me?" Vicki would whisper long after her colleagues had departed at night. "Do your legs work?"

Can you feel heat and light? she would wonder. So she placed a lamp a foot away from his tube. She splayed her hand under its rays, gauging whether it was too hot or not warm enough. When the sway of the candy in the tube felt mechanical to her, as if they would move on their own, she unfurled onto the couch in the corner of the lab, her head next to the automatic kettle. She slept.

The shifting had stopped by the time she awoke three hours later. Cut short in the suspending gelatin agar, the floating bear would no longer move. Vicki tapped on the glass. With long tweezers, she lifted the confectionary out of his prison onto a sterile plate. She brushed the remnant bits off his body, but nothing kicked or twisted. Using a magnifying lens under the lamp, she looked to find thin pathways that stemmed from the bear's belly to its peripheries. Were these colonies? Were these hydraulics? One small black dot was connected to another one more miniature than itself, simple organelles perhaps; both branched around the tiny body to the holes of its eyes, its nubby hands and feet, its pricked ears.

And Vicki apologized to the body. She studied it, turned it over in her hand, put its green corpse close to her ear to listen for a heartbeat, however gaunt. She didn't hear a thing. She breathed— she whispered, "I'm sorry." With formalin in short supply, she dipped the corpse into a bath of liquid nitrogen, placing the frozen shell into a plastic-lined slide case. She cleared a small and reverent space for her poor victim at the bottom of the lowest shelf in the freezer, sniffled because of the stillness of its body before leaving the lab for the night.

But little GB019 danced! Little Kevin danced and moved with an even grace. Where his dead forebears exhibited a rough locomotion, if any, all of them stuck in the slow movement of their tubes, Kevin swung in circles and smooth planes. He shook. He tumbled. The curve of a grin carved into his face or not, he smiled always.

Days ago, after the cold suffering of four other little candies, Vicki had watched carefully for signs of struggle in the new tube. Kevin rested at an incline to the left in the agar gel, cocked just slightly. She stared and sought wiggles of an arm or foot. First, then, there was the spasm of the head, the shaking and the innate need for broad movement in the bear's sticky cell. There was repeated movement and results, and this was a cause for celebration.

So Vicki swelled. She rescued the small bear with padded tweezers and cleaned his face with a swab of distilled water on cotton. There was forever the smile.

She called for pizza again after weeks of the delivery boy's absence. She tugged at the first Kevin's deliberate mandible as he grunted on the lab couch, naked from the waist down. Later, she wrote while the other Kevin sat on a soft bed of cellophane. His namesake gone back and down into the traffic of Cambridge again, the little candy now seemed content to roll around in the clear plastic sheets. Vicki scribbled furiously.

I have named GB019 'Kevin', after the pizza boy, she wrote. Does he respire? If so, how? Is there a GI tract? How does he void? While the sugary bear ramped up and down the clear plastic at her workstation, Vicki could not help but think of sign language, of Koko the knowledgeable gorilla and the primate's small gray kittens.

It was close to dawn now. Vicki yawned frequently. Taking a small Erlenmeyer flask from the corner of her desk, Vicki filled the beaker with stuffed slips of cellophane. She padded the sheets down, crossed her fingers and hoped the bedstead was soft, dropping Kevin from her careful fingers into the flask below. She left the lid off and carried the little bear in her hands to the lab couch, set her alarm, pulled his glass close to her. She napped while Kevin slept, tired like a puppy from a few hours' worth of life already. She hoped he would dance again when she awoke and would be able to remember how she had animated him.

But there was the lab phone to answer.

"Hal?" she asked into the receiver.

Cradled in her hands was the flask, Kevin's sticky paws touching the glass wall, still alive and shimmying. The pinpricks of eyes cut into his head by the Jools Confectionary machines beamed up at his creator. He wiggled and, she believed, he loved her. She carried him with her to the chirping telephone in the corner.

"Hello?" she mumbled. Vicki looked at the time and the date, somewhere close to 9 a.m. on a Saturday and counting. There was a sobbing now. Someone cried and hurt painfully on the other end of the line. Was it April yet on campus?

"The baby," Elizabeth blurted. "Its bones."

After a muffled, staccato explanation, Victoria Clive wept with the trembling voice she tried to soothe.

"Oh, sweetheart," she whispered. "It's not your fault." And Kevin shook. He radiated love. "This could have been any number of things." She stretched out her words like gauze, pulled and wrapped them like a bandage. A red dollop of love sambaed in her hands.

"I'm so sorry," she blubbered. And the Gummi Bear waltzed. "I am so, so sorry."

On her fingers, she felt the quick weight of gooey footsteps as they touched the glass bottom, busy now in a shuffle of turns and swoops.

In her lap, Kevin moved. Perhaps he felt the need to show off his lack of a skeletal frame and his invisibly functioning muscles to the woman who coaxed them both into production. Perhaps he had energy to burn. There was the Red 40 blood he was thankful for, and the sugar-spun neural connections. He danced with the slit smile on his face and his ears to the sky.

In her sister's womb, Vicki's niece or nephew rolled as well. Elizabeth's fetus slept and, when it awoke, kicked. Unlike Kevin in his flask, the child had a skeleton, the spine of which, though, as Vicki learned, was not covered by skin. In the blue and gray images of the child on the ultrasound's display she imagined her sister had seen, Vicki began to trace vertebrae that rippled visibly down the tiny child's back, and how, so oddly, it continued this way down the side of its visible left leg. She could see the soft fetal bone that would lay jagged against the side of the nebulous body. Victoria imagined that Elizabeth's physician had touched her arm, murmured words next to her hurt mind like 'surgery' and 'abnormalities.'

In a laboratory close to the cold Atlantic, Victoria Clive rubbed her wet, slick eyes with her fingertips. She touched the plump skin of the sugary little bear on her table, and she looked for signs of spina bifida on her own sweet son.

"It's still inside of me," her sister whimpered into the phone. Vicki let little Kevin march onto the palm of her hand.

"Liz," Vicki cooed. "Liz." She could imagine the contingencies. 'Spina bifida:' the phrase quivered in her thoughts like Kevin on the lines of her hand. Her niece or nephew's malformed skeleton would require extensive surgery. Even if the surgery was possible, there was no guarantee the child would survive past massive infection, or physical or mental retardation, or both. Lifting the sweet and dancing bear to her eyes, Vicki looked for organs and structures in her own child.

Over the ripples of the Charles and a telephone line, eyes and muscles and a heart and bones kicked in a suspension of amniotic fluid. Where there was just enough space for a femur and the bowing arcs of a tibia and a fibula, a jagged line of misplaced spinal mountains erupted from the skin. In her labs, Vicki could smell how the citric-acid scent of her child blended with carnauba wax.

She believed she could trace the outline of filament bone in the wiggling gelatin.

And in the throbs of the heart that Vicki listened for in her sister's breathing, she heard only a voice.

"What do I do?" she heard. So much hurt in her tone, so much pity and pain together.

In blustery New England, quietly as she could, Victoria Clive licked the writhing back of the Gummi Bear, still moving, still in love with her touch. Her lips kissed the agar-tube child unconditionally, and, across telephone wires, Victoria made every effort to muffle the sound of her teeth.

"You start over, sweetheart," Vicki murmured, still chewing, still moving the bones of her jaw. "You begin again."

Caltrops

You speed up and throw out a couple of them onto the left lane of I-90 West as you drive home one morning, two little gifts of stiff iron spikes for the hotshot with the Bluetooth headset, the complete lack of attention to the road, a blind spot. Just 500 yards ahead, you slow down a bit to hear the 'pop pop pop' of sharp metal gouging into tires. The driver rolls off into the grass median at a crawl, paying full attention now, of course, and you coast happily toward the rest stop as a state cruiser flips on his lights in the eastbound lanes and away from you.

A few days later, in a grocery store parking lot, you leave a present for the woman who has knocked off your side-view mirror with her door, and who doesn't check to see if you're still in the car before she puts her sedan in reverse and creeps in three spots over. After you wedge a caltrop under her tire, you do the same as her and slide over into the next row like a burglar. You wait a good half hour for her to come back out and there she is, huffing it down the aisle with a bag from Macy's under each arm. And then there's the 'pop' of her Goodyear in the hot summer sun and the sound of your engine as it revs to leave before she calls mall security.

At the bright hotel where you work in the nighttime—a three-star that overlooks Boston Harbor—you still haven't told the ladies in Human Resources about the summer you spent learning how to gas weld. (The 'Special Skills' section on the job application was left blank, you remember.) And when you buy another tank of acetylene mix from the cashier at Sears who rings you out each month, he asks what you do with it, and you say, "Modern free-standing installations, mostly," and you slap out five twenties before leaving with another ten cubic feet of gas and the driver's license in your wallet that the cashier didn't ask to see. At home, you build the little works of sharpened origami in solid steel, tiny stars only a hand-width high with four tips: three on the ground and one in the sky, all of them the same length for support. Into the trunk they go with a few left out for the glove compartment, then, like heavy Christmas ornaments in the month of May.

In feudal Japan, you remember, caltrops were used on the bat-tlefields to hobble cavalry horses, stuck into the ground with their spikes pointing toward the sun, placed there to draw troops into a wedge so they'd be easier targets for archers. Centuries later, when the Vietnamese tried to push out the Americans, the little spikes of iron were used by snipers in the jungles; when an enemy stepped on one, they'd jump and yell out in pain and then, 'pop,' a hole would appear after a rifle's report.

During your days spent in Boston, though, while the maids from Port au Prince bleach white queen-sized sheets and restock bottles of citrus conditioner at the hotel, you're at home with a torch and remnant hunks of fuselage plates and old boat struts you can cut down into strips. You weld the little traps into the shape of a tetrahedron, like the jacks from a child's playground game, or a crystal that's fallen from the ceiling of Superman's Fortress of Solitude: whatever will blow out a tire at its tread.

It's at night when you're on the phone to guests who call down from the upper floors with a view of the harbor that you dream of maps and of that stretch of highway between Boston and Seattle, of the asphalt that runs through the northern U.S. like it's trying to avoid hot weather and Baptists. Between explanations to the hotel guests, from the CFO in the penthouse to the nineteen-year-olds flying out from Logan the next morning, that, no, you don't know the number to any escort services in the nearby vicinity, you can't help but get that look on your face as you drift out onto the Mass Turnpike in a daydream.

From behind the counter in your suit and tie and name tag, there's the hope of vacation days come summertime, when you'll load up the car with a bag of sandwiches and a backseat full of iron and steel spikes. Out in front of you will be nothing but painted concrete and Ohio and Montana and every car and small injustice in between, and you'll feel like Johnny Appleseed if he'd owned a soldering iron, or the man who brought kudzu to the highways of America.

The View from Pittsburgh

Eileen had always wanted to make love on a piano, to have the keys notch into the meat of her ass as someone pumped away at her atop them, and so she bought one, an old walnut upright with a cracked soundboard and a droopy leg. She polished the old, familiar thing daily and worked to fix it and herself up someday so that only middle C would fit between her cheeks when it happened. She aimed to reduce herself—that was her mother's word, 'reduce'—down to the point where her thighs didn't meet at the top, down into a frame that her younger brother had once labeled, without him knowing she was in earshot, as a woman's "gap."

The piano had been her mother's once, actually, sold after her death to the first Craigslist buyer who answered the ad and paid in cash. He skidded into the driveway in a mottled red Ford pickup and a stained V-neck, and he paid her $100 for the instrument. It was the last large object of her mother's that Eileen had sold after the funeral, gone after the dressers, the secretary, the ottoman, and the five separate end tables. The piano even stayed after the sale of the oversized horse painting, the landscape that once hung above the bed that Eileen's mother had hibernated in for those two years. Her mother, Babs, paid $1500 for the twelve square feet of a field scene with the horse in the middle of it, and she'd fixed it above the bed with a single nail and a hammer and a stretch of wire. Once the painting stopped swaying on the wall, Babs climbed into her wardrobe of nightgowns and stayed mostly in them for the last two years of her life.

But Eileen didn't recognize the piano once she bought it back, not even as she was helping to load it into the cargo bed. She surprised the seller, a clean-cut man with a blond fade, by helping him lift it into the back of the commercial pickup she'd rented that morning. The white truck had the 'Rent Me Today!' suggestion professionally spray-painted onto both sides and onto its tailgate, and Eileen followed the suggestion with a phone call. She pulled into the man's driveway at two that afternoon, the time they agreed upon, sized him up and down and saw what she liked. She surprised him when he asked her if she brought anyone to help lift the piano into the rig, and she said, no, it was just her, and so the blond man had called over to his neighbor from across the street and asked for his help.

"I think we've got this," Eileen said, "the four of us. We can do this." And because the neighbor brought the contractor he'd been speaking with in the driveway, they did.

To achieve her 'gap,' Eileen had been busy at the gym, working on her deadlifts and her farmer's squats, lumping herself and a pair of dumbbells on an invisible track along the gym's tiled floors. The three men laughed, the blond man and his neighbor and the grizzly contractor, but they shot each other a glance in the middle of the lift of the piano. It was the neighbor on one end with the older man, the one with the pencil behind his ear, who lifted more than he looked like he could hold, and it was Eileen and the blond seller on the other end. And then it was Eileen's thighs touching the blond man's thighs, and Eileen's flexed arm touching his flexed arm, and there was the grunt made at the end of a short burst of lust that the both of them produced in that final lift, and that had been enough for Eileen. She'd surprised the three and thanked the neighbor and the old contractor by bending well over in gratitude and letting their eyes jut down to her cleavage as she opened her purse. She paid the seller his $50 cash and then realized in the man's driveway that the piano had once belonged to Babs—a sticker from the moving company had triggered whatever was necessary in her memory—and the afternoon was shot and all but dead.

At home, she remembered, there was a photograph she kept from her mother's collection of things. It was an old sepia toned portrait, taken of Babs when she had muscle and orneriness left in her, back when you could see the veins in her arms. She was wearing a gingham dress of white and black, more black than anything, really, and she'd been splayed over the lid of her piano, her arms hunched over in a gorilla's pose, and she was giving hell to whomever was taking the photograph with her beautifully scowling face and her lips that were just beginning to creep up into a smirk. It was a gorgeous photo, Eileen knew this, and this was why she'd kept it after Babs' death. Until she sold the piano, the photograph in its frame had stayed right next to the lamp her mother had once used to read sheet music.

Frustrated by the return of the piano and the weight of the fact that she bought back what she had once sold, Eileen drove home without a plan to get the old piano out of the payload. She could loosen the ratchet ties herself, of course, the ones she fixed on her own after the men near the street helped her swing the piano into place. It was stationary, she knew, and it was secure, and the piano wasn't going to go anywhere as she bounced down Route 12 toward home and the rest of the hills in northeast Pennsylvania. She ran through her options on the drive. She did math on a deadline, keeping that twenty-four-hour rental agreement at the front of the word problem, but it was useless.

There was Cavanaugh, who worked the long hours landscaping in the day and who wouldn't be home until late that night, she reasoned. And there was Mrs. Farnstein, the adjacent septuagenarian, who would hem and haw on Eileen's behalf if she wanted it, but there wasn't a fiber of muscle tissue left in the woman. And then there was the Godbey family's teenager, a sixteen-year-old who was raised thin and whom she'd caught with a pair of binoculars several times over, distracting enough to the point where she finally had to install wooden slat blinds on the south windows of her bedroom. If he wanted to spy on her, she reasoned, he'd have to set up a deer blind in the trees of the east lawn, where the open windows were fixed. But his parents were gone for the weekend, and Eileen wasn't going to give hope to a kid who couldn't install a deer blind or hide an old ladder behind a tree.

"And he's got about as much muscle as Mrs. Farnstein," Eileen said on the drive, to no one but herself.

So there it was: another driveway (her own) but with a familiar piano (the same; her mother's), and another three feet of air between the ground and the bed of the truck. Despite the muscle she'd put on at the gym, Eileen caught herself thinking, *I could use a strong man right now*. But there was nothing but the sounds of the neighborhood to help her lower the piano to the ground. There were birds chirping in an unhelpful language, and there was a woodpecker in there somewhere, and there was always the sound of someone mowing a lawn in the daylight hours, but no great assistance was coming.

Between the time she jumped down from the cab of the truck to the time she dragged out the mattress from the twin bed in the guest room, Eileen went through all of her local contacts in her head. She wouldn't call anyone from the old stenography pool or from the office, not on her day off. She wouldn't call her friends on a hunt for their husbands because they all worked and because the phone conversations wouldn't pay out anyway. So that just left the mattress and the hope that it would catch the piano when she shoved it out of the back of the truck.

In that second before the piano fell to the twin mattress, Eileen remembered the $50-dollar bill and the blond man and his pretty haircut. She hadn't picked up enough speed as she railed the piano out onto the gate of the truck bed, and so the wooden cabinet of the instrument landed hard on its corner, in spite of all the padding below it, but she did remember for some reason that his haircut was called an "Ivy League fade," and that it was parted hard to one side, and that she had seen the name for it in a magazine that was left on the coffee table at her salon. It was a younger man's haircut, built for someone with the confidence of college around him, and as the piano bounced twice and landed on its back with a thud, almost to where the lip of the bed couldn't stop it from toppling, Eileen wondered how well the blond man loved his wife.

The divorce made sense at the time. Eileen and Cavanaugh had been with each other since their shared twenty-first birthdays, and the stopwatch on what was still good for both of them seemed like it was winding down. She had her stake now in the transcription group, as it was growing and still young and hungry, like she'd been once. She had seen the fading light at the end of stenography as a discipline and as a skill, and now she was traveling and glad-handing for the largest transcription service in northeast Pennsylvania. She typed fewer words and donned the earphones less than ever now, and she had more time on her hands to notice what was missing from her life.

And Cavanaugh was the same: ever since he'd bought the landscaping company from the developers he worked for, there was more pride in what he did, but there was less of him at the house and less of him ready for the pent-up energy Eileen had accumulated in the day. When he would come home, she would grab him from the door and direct him up the stairs and to their bed, or sometimes to the plush couch in the living room, reminding herself in the middle of things, when Cavanaugh's head was between her thighs, that she made a plate for him that was now sitting in the fridge but one that would keep just a while longer.

And that had been the case for the pair of them, right up until Eileen announced her intention to move Babs into the house: a double-income home with no kids and too much time on one set of hands, too little on the other. The split was quick and understood by both parties as a necessity if they were still going to get along, and it was the envy of their divorced friends. Eileen and Cavanaugh were still amicable, still lovers when they had the time and spirit, and Eileen now had something and someone to fill the gaps in her schedule. There had been no children for the married couple to keep them together artificially, fortunately, but Babs would need enough attention so that it would seem like a home with a child at times.

Eileen still depended on Cavanaugh, though, for the occasional hair of advice.

"Where in the hell should I hide her pills?" she asked him once, calling because she knew he would be home at that time of night.

He seemed to chew it over genuinely, she believed, and he responded, "That high shelf in the garage would be fine. Plant an old wrench in front of a cardboard box, and she'll never investigate it. I promise that." And Eileen had, and Babs had never found her pills, despite several attempts at looking on those Sunday nights, when Eileen would refill her mother's tiny boxes of individual doses for the upcoming week. She knew this was now what Cavanaugh was capable of, if not direct help in a home they shared, and that she had made the right decision not to ask him to stay before Babs arrived from Pittsburgh. But still, she missed the regular thrush of those fine hairs on his stomach as she laid into him at night.

She remembered how the mountains and greens around Wilkes-Barre had been lovely enough for them as children, and how they'd reasoned this separately as individuals, and so it was good enough for them as adults. Eileen's father was offered a comfortable promotion at the Farmer's Insurance corporate offices in Pittsburgh so many years ago, but he wound up convincing only Babs and Eileen's brother, Nathan, in coming with him, and not Eileen. Instead, the young woman, fresh out of high school, chose to stay in the hills and the lakes around Wilkes-Barre, and she found comfort in the rhythm of life in the courts and on the stenotypes she sat down with each day. Her fingers were kept busy, and the legal proceedings were dotted with enough acts of arson and theft to stay interesting.

And then she met Cavanaugh, the young man with the last name for a first name, who maintained the city grounds and planted trees in the spring. At the bowling lanes their separate tribes both frequented on the weekends, they would acknowledge the occasions when they'd seen each other during the days, she coming down the courtroom steps and he at the foot of them, planting shrubs into lines. Eileen had been more interested in sneaking the beer from the counter instead of how many strikes she'd accumulated. And there was Cavanaugh, who had his own bottle and who was of the legal age already, and she liked the looks of him enough to ask for a sip that didn't come from a plastic cup that had to be hidden from the management. When the lights finally dimmed on each of the lanes, long after Eileen's group from the courthouse had gone, she walked with Cavanaugh back to his truck and had climbed into the driver's side door while pulling on him to follow her. That night, in the only vehicle left in the lanes' parking lot, she pulled the rough man's hands over the lip of her dress and under it, up to where he could feel how much she enjoyed his touch.

Years later, though, there was Babs, the flightless bird who nonetheless believed she could fly on her combination of controlled-release opioids, blood thinners, and Wild Turkey, and there was the phone call to Eileen when she'd pushed back up from the concussion, and the long drive west to Pittsburgh to retrieve her, and then that had been the end of Cavanaugh's warm touch each night.

"Well, can't Nathan move in with her?" he asked, almost pleading.

"He can't stand her, and she can't stand him," she said to her husband. "They're just too much alike to ever live with each other."

And this was true. Eileen's younger brother, Nathan, was the image of her father as she'd seen him in portraits from his youth, but her sibling contained in himself Babs' love of possessions, her staggering mood swings, and her selfishness. The selfishness helped him on the lacrosse fields of junior high and high school, Eileen remembered, and Nathan's bravado carried him through college and optometry school, where he learned how to make money and keep it. The night they buried their father, when the question about Babs' future wasn't quite ready to be spoken, Eileen and Nathan got drunk with his friends and, when the boys and their young wives had gone home, Nathan plopped down on the couch next to his sister and said, "Did you know that Pennsylvania is one of the states where children can be held accountable for their parents' medical debts?"

Eileen watched him shake his head back and forth, saying "no" to a question that hadn't been asked, and so she started to nod on her own and on the wave of the vodka tonics she'd downed after the service.

"When the time comes, then," she said, "we'll see what needs to happen, and we'll just do it." While she saw that this meant to Nathan that the responsibility for his mother would never be his, Eileen saw a future where Babs would one day move in with her, or vice versa, and she hoped that this day wouldn't happen for a long, long time.

Three years later, with Cavanaugh next to her for the duration of it, and with Nathan freshly divorced, Eileen visited on the weekends to Pittsburgh and watched as Babs drummed herself down into a wreck of co-dependency. It had started with a slip of the ankle in a church parking lot, on a curb she wasn't used to, and a broken foot. Babs found herself in love with the opioids her doctors prescribed her and in deep need of the benzodiazepines that accompanied the narcotics. The physical therapy for the foot that her physician signed her up for was never taken advantage of. The pain was too much, Babs claimed—she just didn't have the energy—but the there was always the energy needed to get herself back to her doctor for a recheck and a refill of the meds. And so the problem with the foot became a problem of the leg, and Eileen watched her mother develop a limp and a stumble and a visible disability that would always need a prescription and, then, a tag for the handicapped spots at the store.

"You need physical therapy, mom," Eileen would say, "if you ever want to get better."

But Babs' response was always the same: "I'll ask my doctor about it next time."

The young physician, a resident who was still figuring out the hospital's human resources website, never did force the issue or hold her scrips back, though. Like the case with Babs, his patient, there just wasn't the energy.

So the phone call that Babs made to her daughter one day was as inevitable as anything in this world. An old woman tripped and fell, and a young woman picked her up. A move across the state was made, and when Babs' boxes came, Cavanaugh's things were already gone, the space he once occupied still warm and now waiting for her. The sounds in the house changed, too. At night, where there was once the thump of a head against a backboard or a moan in the night, there was now the lurch of the old woman downstairs and, if one listened hard enough to the second floor of the house, the gentle hum of a vibrator that was being used more often these days.

Her brother had learned that phrase—'gap'—from the internet. She assumed it was a meme because, unless he was in front of clients, Nathan talked in memes. When he wasn't busy recommending protective coatings for his patients' glasses, he would pay attention to these things, clicking from site to site to site. Nathan wouldn't just pepper his speech with these phrases, either; he tossed in great garlic cloves of the memes into his conversations. Nothing was funny, but it could be LOL. Nothing needed a rational disagreement when it could be dismissed with a "The stupid: it hurts" from him.

This was Nathan, but on the evening of Babs' viewing, after the siblings had greeted family friends and the people who knew Babs in her waning years, Nathan hadn't even bothered to recognize his sister and her ex-husband as the drivers of the car he was riding in. While Eileen and Cavanaugh assumed they were heading for Nathan's house, plans had already been made in the young optometrist's head.

"Need me a motherfucking milkshake," he mumbled to himself. "Chocolate."

"Were you drinking during the memorial service," asked Cavanaugh, grinning, "or was this still all from before?"

Eileen drove and saw her brother's swaying neck in the rearview. She caught him looking up at the roof of the car for answers, wafting out the warm puffs of Wild Turkey on his breath that had been downed earlier.

"Why not both?" Nathan said. He giggled.

Cavanaugh had of course come with Eileen when she asked. He could set his own hours, Eileen reasoned, but it was still good that he agreed so quickly when she told him about Babs' blood clot and the embolism that had finished the clot's hard work. While Cavanaugh hadn't been around recently, he'd been there just minutes after Eileen had left the bad news on his voicemail. He looked odd, she believed, in the black suit and the white shirt underneath, but the tie fit him. And now he was here in the front seat with her, in the rungs of Pittsburgh, protecting her from the terrible things Nathan would let slip from his mouth that night.

The trio of mourners was almost to the custard shop when Eileen rolled the car up to a stop sign, the one that a young runner was passing at that very moment.

"Mmm mmm mmm!" Nathan hummed, as though he was settling down to a hot breakfast. "Love me a woman with a gap!"

In the periphery, and with the windows down, Eileen knew that the blonde runner had stopped to catch her breath. She paused at the stop sign to hold her footing, and she began stretching her calves on the sidewalk, giving the travelers in the car just enough time to see whatever they could see. Under whatever was playing in her headphones, the runner either couldn't hear Nathan's remark or she just didn't care.

"She is fit, I'll say that," said Cavanaugh, grinning back at Nathan. Eileen blushed and turned her head toward the intersection and the custard shop, but curiosity got the best of her.

"Wait, what did you say?" she asked. "What's 'a gap'?"

Cavanaugh said nothing but smiled sheepishly in the passenger seat, and Nathan piped up almost immediately, catching himself after having done something chauvinistic in front of his sister.

"It's a joke, Eileen. Didn't mean a thing."

"Tell me," she said. It was Cavanaugh's turn to twist his head away from the conversation. "I want in on the joke."

The car thrummed into the parking lot of Creedy's Custard, one of the few franchises from the Pittsburgh suburbs that had managed to creep its way from the countryside into the city limits. It sold milkshakes and great, heaping tubs of frozen custard and blended toppings. To Eileen, it made the coastal state of Pennsylvania feel awfully like the Midwest.

"It means when there's space at the top of a girl's thighs," Nathan mumbled. "Low body fat and muscly quads, you know?" There was a pause as the trio watched an old Chevrolet back out of a coveted parking spot. "I don't know if there's the equivalent for guys. Cav?"

And Cavanaugh turned his head back for just a moment. "Sure," he said. "Guys can have a gap. Why not?"

The boys dodged her as best they could while ordering and eating their cold custards. They looked almost relieved when Eileen asked about the plans for the next day, about what they would do with the visitors if there were any.

"Funeral's at eleven, right?" she said. "So what time do you want to drive over, Nate? Or do you even want to drive over together?"

"Yeah, yeah," he said. "Three musketeers style. What time do you want me over there?" Eileen turned to get Cavanaugh's opinion on the matter again, but he was looking at the low-cut shirt on the girl at the window. The young woman was leaning over and counting back change for a small boy who'd paid for his custard with his mother's fan of dollar bills.

"Ten?" she said. "10:30? Cav? What time do you want to leave?"

And Cavanaugh swiveled back around. "What? Yeah, anytime is fine."

Eileen wondered if there was a space between the thighs of the girl who worked at the window at Creedy's, and when Cavanaugh and Nathan ordered their milkshakes, Eileen declined, saying she wasn't in the mood for dessert. Still, the smell of the sweet and sour milk played in the warm night air, and she shook her head at her own notions.

Later, when Nathan was passed out in the back from either too much custard or bourbon or sadness or relief at his mother's passing, it was just Eileen and Cavanaugh who were conscious. Eileen was still driving, and Cavanaugh was still awake, but it took a swift turn into the parking lot of a vintage clothing store to jar him into full attention.

"I need a dress," said Eileen, more to the dashboard and less to Cavanaugh as she opened the car door.

Cavanaugh climbed out after her on his side, looking half back at Nathan and half at Eileen. "You brought one for tomorrow, remember?" he said. "That black and blue number?"

Eileen didn't acknowledge this but instead pushed through the door to the shop. Inside, there were enough pleated slacks and broaches and feathered pillbox hats on the shelves and racks to supply most people looking for a costume. But like a lot of women her age or younger, Eileen was there for proper clothes. She needed to look strong, she believed, in front of Cavanaugh and Nathan, and even Babs tomorrow.

And then Cavanaugh came in behind her and muttered a 'wow' upon seeing the rows of clothes and gloves. Eileen had always admired this trait of her ex-husband: his penchant for the timeliness of things, his rejection of fads and what was in vogue at the moment. She remembered, for example, the way he always wore his plaid shirts, with the cuffs rolled up to just above his elbows. While she watched this trend emerge among the young men who attended the local colleges in Wilkes-Barre, the style that Cavanaugh favored had never waxed or waned. It instead always came with a sense of practicality, like with the canvas pants he wore that lasted longer than the dungarees Eileen had given him. To her, it seemed like Cavanaugh would fit best in a Brooklyn studio some days, or in a daguerrotype of a silver miners' village from the 1840s in others.

"What about this one?" she asked, holding up a dark blue dress. It came with a sash, and there was a string of costume pearls that would go well with it all.

"Looks a lot like the one you brought," he shrugged. "But it's fine."

Eileen fit the dress back on the line and moved closer to Cavanaugh. She stopped herself and cocked her head toward the cash register at the front of the store, searching for the Gil Evgren-type salesgirl that she'd have to compete against for his attention, as well, but she found only a young hipster with a mustache and a crossword puzzle at his fingertips. She stood next to her ex-husband—that was such a horrible prefix to use when she still loved the man—and took his cologne in. He smelled of bay rum that had been spent on thanking Babs' old neighbors for coming to the viewing, whispering softly to them that he'd see them again at the funeral. She nuzzled close to the man, thinking of Babs and the empty house they would have to sleep in that night. She wanted to bury herself in the battling perfumes of the clothes on the racks, and she wanted to wash herself clean of the last two weeks' worth of hospital visits, quiet consultations with the attending physicians, and funeral arrangements. That would be over tomorrow, though, she told herself, and then there would be the new war on Babs' things to wage.

"See here?" Cavanaugh asked. He began pulling out a checkered dress, a familiar black-and-white gingham that was dark and rich in its pattern. "Would this work?" And he held it up to Eileen, who pulled it close to her body. She looked for a size on the tag and, finding nothing, smiled at Cavanaugh and took the dress to the changing room in the back.

"I've always liked that type of dress," he whispered, grinning as she took off toward the rear of the shop.

The room was little more than a closet, a partition of drywall on three sides and a jungle-green curtain on a rod she could pull to cover the front. She unzipped her dress after closing the curtain and placed the dark fabric on an adjacent hook. Next to her was the mirror, a full-length piece of glass that reflected her body and her underwear back to her. She stared at herself and rearranged her bra, moving her breasts back and forth until they were comfortable again. She sighed at her stomach and the places it lobed off at the sides. She stared at her hips and at the place between them where there would one day be a gap, if only she could reduce the fat there.

That was her mother's word, wasn't it? 'Reduce?' As in, *That man of yours? 'Cabana?'*

"Cavanaugh," Eileen had said. The woman knew damn well her fiancé's name.

Cavanaugh might not go for the more full-bodied frames like mine, Babs offered. *You might work to reduce some of your baby fat. Hit the machines down at the 'Y' and sweat out the fat.*

But then Cavanaugh appeared in the changing room, slipping himself into Eileen's present and in between the curtain and the wall, as though the sheet was heavy and made of chain mail.

"Don't mind me," he said, smiling at her. "The fellow at the front is busy with his paper."

Eileen drew him close and smiled back at him. Babs' death? Her mother's passing? This was a relief for the man, who'd always roughed it out with the woman when he came over to visit. When Babs was living with Eileen, Cavanaugh could barely make it to the five-minute mark when he called on Eileen at the house. There were pleasantries to be made and inquiries on Babs' health, but that was as far as Cavanaugh's politeness took him. The rest was a series of jibes and snips from the mother of the woman he loved, and the divorce, he and Eileen reasoned, was a contingency plan for the future and every year Babs stayed alive.

"Here, let me help," he said, taking the gingham dress down from the hook. He unzipped it and fitted it over Eileen's head. She took it, slid into it, and started checking for the fit. Aside from a small space of extra material in the shoulders, it matched her torso and hips just fine, almost to where Cavanaugh guessed. "See?" he asked. "Let's check you out."

Eileen zipped herself up and found slightly less slack now on the sides. It slimmed her and felt snug but not too much so.

"This just might work," she said, smoothing down the black pleats and lines that were checkered with white. She thought of her mother and whether or not the woman would approve of the dress as appropriate wear for her funeral, and she remembered a photograph of Babs from years ago as Cavanaugh's hands reached gently for her, one to the nape of her neck and one to the scoop of her breasts. "Yes, I think it just might."

Summers after the funeral, there was now the piano to contend with, yet again, and Eileen wondered if she had the strength to lift the damn thing back into place from where it rested on the driveway.

She'd been busy since leaving Pittsburgh. In between phone calls with Babs' insurance reps and the hospital's accounts office, Eileen lived with the free weights right next to her station. She dragged a sturdy wooden chair up from her basement, one that her father had given her one weekend before he and Babs had left for western Pennsylvania those years ago. It was a heavy thing, solid and well built, and this is where Eileen sat with her dumbbells as her transcription recordings played in the background.

She lifted. She moved her dumbbells up and down rhythmically, powering them up and then lowering them down in those spaces where the voice on the recording paused itself for "umms" and "okays." She built muscle while she worked at her desk at home, and, when she wasn't there, she was at the gym, catching the eye of the lunkheads as she snatched barbells up from the ground. She wasn't lifting what the men were lifting, but she was grabbing their attention.

The piano, though, was another story. She stared down at her legs, at her quadriceps that had gained muscle and lost only a little bit of fat, and, here, in the middle of her driveway, she put one hand between her legs to feel how her thighs had thinned away from each other, if at all. There was still the soft padding, although there was less of it now, but this didn't stop her from cursing her brother's offhand remark.

"Fuck you, Nate," she spat. There was no one there to see the reductions and the months of hard work.

For a minute, Eileen retreated into the house. The first room on the left through the garage had been Babs', and it was mostly empty now. There was the space in the corner where that damn piano would fit into again, and there were two boxes: one that was filled with Babs' magazines and headphones and AV cables, and a collection of unused lightbulbs still in their boxes, and there was another box that Eileen had purchased, one that was filled with the flat, black boards and black screws that would someday become an entertainment stand. She didn't know what she was going to put on the thing. It would either be Babs' old television or Babs' record player and a case of her 45s; she wasn't sure just yet.

But at the top of the box, Eileen spied the photograph. It was the portrait of her mother, the one where she was wearing the black-and-white checkered dress and the stern look on her face, with her strong arms on the top of the heavy piano. And Eileen believed right then that Babs had once loved and had once moved that piano from an unknown point A to an unknown point B, had been capable of such a thing, and so she decided to move the instrument herself. There might not be another strong set of arms in the neighborhood, and there might not be Cavanaugh right now, but there was always herself.

Outside, the light was fading. The wooden lid of the piano was lying on the ground, so Eileen scooted the heavy thing back onto the soft pallet of the mattress, and then she crouched down and shoved. At first, the mattress itself moved, taking the piano with it over the rough concrete of Eileen's driveway, but then it caught on a lip of gravel, and then the piano slid over the mattress's side. If there were steps to this process, this would have been the first, but there was the harder, more difficult step to get to right now, while Eileen still had the energy in her.

Lifting from her legs, with her thighs piqued and touching the backs of her calves, with her hands gripping the underside of the piano's worn lid, Eileen squeezed. She contracted her muscles and lifted with her back, feeling the rock of the driveway below her trainers, and she continued to squeeze.

"You are a fucking sex toy," she grunted at the thing, each syllable a strain. "Get the fuck up!"

And it did. The arc of the lift almost caught her near the very end, when the piano's wheels started to slip, but they caught onto something down there and held. But it was done now, and all that was left was the cleanup.

First, Eileen shoved the piano over the rest of the driveway's length, pushing it into the garage and over the small wooden line where the screen door between the garage and the house's interior rested. Next, she pushed the great instrument into the corner where it once slept, hauling it over the slate tiles on her floor where Babs used to tread. And it would stay in the corner, she thought, until maybe forever.

Panting, she took her phone from her pocket and dialed Cavanaugh, knowing he wouldn't pick up in the late afternoon. There was still an hour left in the workday, and he would be spending it with a bag of mulch that needed to be spread around the base of a tree, or with a power washer and facing the aluminum siding of a HUD apartment a few neighborhoods over.

"Hey, there," he said, coughing.

Eileen sighed, "You're not working?"

Cavanaugh cleared his throat again and said, "Almost done, actually. We thought we'd get done sooner rather than later on account of the clouds going dark."

Eileen stepped over the window of the room where her mother once lived and looked out toward the sky. It was gray and getting grayer, and she moved toward the piano, stopping now to take off the worn jeans she'd had on since that morning. She let them rest on the slate tiles below.

"Want to come over?" she asked. "It'd be nice to see you."

There was a hesitation there, a second spent too long on a reply. But Eileen held the phone in the crook of one shoulder and moved her underwear down below her knees, then let them fall to where the jeans slumped.

"Mind if I get a shower first?" he asked.

"The water's just as warm over here," Eileen said quickly. "You come on over when you're done."

If she could hear a smile, Eileen would hear it right then. "That I can do," she heard. "See you soon."

Wearing just the shirt and her sports bra underneath it, Eileen went over to the corner of her mother's room—she still thought of the tiny bedroom as such, but the feeling was fading more and more these days—and found in the corner the photograph of Babs above her old piano, her arms hunched over in a pose that showed off the muscle she'd had at the time. She saw her mother's dress and, remembering its familiarity, decided she'd have enough time to change into its vintage sister before Cavanaugh arrived, time enough to test the taut strings and the worn keys of the piano on her flesh.

The Echoless

Seth wakes to the sound of his son screaming in waves of volume from behind him, into the hairs at the nape of his neck. Outside the family van, the sunlight from the garage door windows hits him in the face like a ray gun, and, in between Cody's gasps for air, Seth feels the close reverb of his boy's sobs as they bounce around him in the vehicle. They come at him from the glass of the driver's side door, the dashboard, the visors above his head. In this small plastic and metal box, he is assailed by sound.

Out through the garage, in between the thrums of his son's wails, he watches the divorcée from next door jog past his driveway on her pre-breakfast run. It is morning. Seth knows this as he comes to, but this knowledge and the volume of the sobbing behind him are the only certain things right now.

Below where his drool and his tears river together, Cody's chest bumps up against the black, five-point restraint of his car seat. How long has he been like this? In between where the buckle stretches against his son's cries, Seth sees old flecks of applesauce have creviced their way into the harness. He doesn't know how many hours he's been asleep in front of the steering wheel, but he knows this is the first time he's brought a passenger with him in the nighttime.

"Hey, buddy!" Seth sing-songs, undoing his own seatbelt. "I'm here, I'm here," he hums. He pushes open the driver's side door and leaves it ajar while he flips open Cody's. On the floor behind his seat, below his son's tears, Seth sees the overturned Cheerios and a copy of *Little Blue Truck* with the dirty imprints of his toddler's shoes on the cover.

"We're going to be okay," he says to the boy, who looks up at Seth with what looks like relief. "We are going...to be...okay." While fiddling with Cody's belt, Seth looks overhead and flicks the interior light so that it turns off and will stay off, even with the doors to the car still open.

The seatbelt and straps finally released, Seth pulls Cody close to his body. He holds his son in his arm, puts his child's ear close to his heart and keeps him there, swinging him back and forth in place. Around them, the garage fills with the volume of his son's cries. A dog barks outside. A car driving past changes gears, and the space around them starts to feel cold on his exposed flesh.

"How in the hell?" Seth asks the floor, staring down now at his pelvis and the lonely pair of plaid boxers that covers it. Cody doesn't have an answer for him, though, about why they're both in the car and why Seth has no memory of putting them there. At the hunk of skin on his back, he feels his son pulling on the fat of his torso, clenching his fist and opening it, clenching and opening like a heartbeat.

Inside the house and away from the garage, his boy quiet, finally, the kitchen is clean and untouched. This is a good and certain thing, too: that he's not tried to make breakfast for his son, whatever it might have been, that he hasn't touched the stove or the toaster, or anything else that can heat up and burn.

Seth kisses the blonde down on the boy's head and asks, "Breakfast?" His son's hands keep time gripping and closing, and so he repeats himself, snapping his fingers as he talks. "Hey, buddy. Want breakfast?"

Cody breaks his tic and looks up at his father, nodding his head before returning to Seth's cold chest. How long had they been in the garage?

Making coffee with his son sitting next to him on the counter, he thinks about what could have been. What if Seth had brought the keys with him into the car? Or what if he had driven out in his sleep? What if he had crashed? Cody points to the fridge and squeezes his fingers into fists like those of a gorilla's, his sign for 'milk.' He begins to cry, and Seth obliges, pouring the milk from the jug into a large measuring glass before placing it in the microwave and hitting the 'tea' option.

"Is he okay?"

Rachel. Somewhere in between her deep sleep and the daylight, they've woken her up.

"I think so," Seth says, arching his back, trying to look composed. "I'm making him some honey milk to get him started." At the table, in his plastic seat now, Cody heaves his chest back and forth, staring between Seth and the microwave, between his father and the countertop, his eyes flitting like an oscilloscope.

They've talked about this. About the sleepwalking and the conversations in the night. His condition's never been violent—Rachel and Seth agree on this, and Seth knows they never would've been married if it had been—but it's always been a surprise as to just what Seth might dream and act out while asleep. When it was just the two of them, they remember, long before Cody and when they'd just moved into the apartment near campus, there had been the first incident they'd shared as a couple: voices, panic, a knife.

When they have guests over to the house now, this is how Rachel tells the story: in the middle of their first autumn together, she'd woken in the night to the sound of Seth bargaining for their lives.

This was after they'd rented the place, after she'd started the nursing program and after Seth had been funded on the research grant from the Physics department. After they'd been sleeping together for a long time, after the sleep was almost as good and refreshing as the sex. Not quite, but close, and so they'd started to learn each other's sleep habits.

Rachel, for example, slept deeply and always on her back. In Seth, she'd found a body upon which to prop her legs as she pitched them up while asleep. Seth asked her once, "How do you sleep so hard? How are you able to pass out once you hit the pillow?"

"Clear conscience," she replied, smirking and closing her eyes.

On the night of the disturbance, though, the air thick around her head, something had woken Rachel from that pit, and she'd seen Seth at the window, busy in dialogue with someone else who was in the room with them. He was close to her side of the bed and was keeping his voice down, but he was begging.

"Please," he said. "Just leave."

Rachel roused and heard this word, "please," this request. For what, though, she wasn't sure, but her eyes were now open and she was listening.

"No need for this," Seth said. "You don't have to do it."

We are being robbed, Rachel believed. *We shouldn't have left the windows unlocked downstairs. We are dead if we don't save ourselves.*

And so Rachel had leapt out of bed for the kitchen downstairs, for the great butcher knife a friend bought them as a housewarming present. It was stainless steel, and it just might save them, she thought. But at the foot of the foyer, when she listened back up for whatever the intruders were doing to her poor boyfriend, Rachel heard nothing. No whispers, no thuds of bodies. No cries for help.

She took the steps back up one at a time, listening for the squeaks in the dark she knew would give away her position on the stairs.

"Yeah," she heard. "Of course. Why wouldn't you?" A small chuckle at the end. Seth's voice.

When she peeked around the door, knife in hand, there was her boyfriend, sitting on the edge of the bed now, nodding.

"We owe you. No contest there, right?" he asked. But Seth was alone.

Rachel remembered the superstitions about waking somnambulists. You weren't supposed to, the tales told her, but the fear was gone now that the knife was there. Just in case.

"Seth?" Rachel asked the gloom.

"Yeah, babe?" Seth responded. She hoped he was talking to her then, and not to another woman in his dream.

"Who are you talking to?"

There was a pause in this, like Seth was thinking about the question. Like he was chewing it slowly.

"The band, you know?" Seth moved his arm and waved his hand. Like nothing could have been more obvious. "Nobody paid them."

"The band?"

"They played the set," Seth explained, the words rolling quietly out of him, "and nobody paid them afterward. I'd be mad, too."

And then Seth dropped back down on the bed. He curled his body and mashed his face into the memory foam pillow. They'd bought the matching pillows together, he and Rachel, their first investment as a couple. Despite the humidity, he snored softly in the dark of their room.

In the morning, when Rachel woke second and grinned at her yawning boyfriend, she tugged on his shoulder and asked him about the band from the night before.

"The hell are you talking about?" Seth grumbled, slumping back into the sheets.

And then he'd woken again and stared at the space behind her, toward her nightstand and her two glasses of water, and he opened his mouth to ask a question about the glinting kitchen knife she'd come back with just hours before.

The drive to work after waking up in the garage is angry and just as filled with sobs as what roused Seth that morning in his driver's seat. Cody stares out his window behind his parents and will quiet down at times, will stare back at them and start the whole sobbing set over in a cycle. He holds a plastic dump truck in his hands and squints at the sunlight through his tears.

"See, you're acting all over again as if this is something I can control," Seth says under the wailing. He weaves around a lumbering SUV in the left lane. Its driver is on the phone and running ten miles below the speed limit.

"You damn well can control it," Rachel says between her son's breaths. "You just need sleep. You need to go to bed on time. We have talked about this."

Cars behind Seth perform the same sweep from the left to the right lane and around the SUV. They move in a wave around the caller.

"Going to bed on time doesn't give me a lot of chances to get to the corporate requests," he tells her. "Which I hate doing, by the way."

At the university, all the attention is now on the new testing chamber in the Physics department that Seth has dubbed 'The Room.' It's never about Seth's work, just the Room and its design, its potential.

The Room, he wants to tell each of the private start-ups, is just like any other acoustic anechoic chamber out there, except that it's a bit quieter than the average rig. It just so happens that the university at Mesa del Sol has paid for its own version that can dip down into the negative decibels, can stifle sound and eat the very idea of volume up, and that's where Seth's work is with the microphones he researches and develops.

"I do this every time you go away for a conference," Rachel says, "and I can put Cody to bed by myself this week while you finish at school." Behind them, the SUV driver has gotten off the phone and is wanting her place back in the line, and Cody is sniffling and coming down from his outburst. "You just need to come to bed and get your full eight."

Seth yawns at the wheel. They agree on this.

Near the campus is Cody's daycare, a program run by the Jesuits that gets top marks each time they pop up for state accreditation. Neither Seth nor Rachel are Catholic, but they don't mind if Cody sees a few crucifixes while he's being taught his letters and how to be a little citizen in his overalls.

The scare of that morning seemingly not quite gone from his mind, Cody starts to cry again as Rachel pulls him out of his car seat. This happens each Monday morning, the crying—each morning, really, and each day of Seth's life since their son's birth almost fourteen months ago—but there's good reason for it today.

"Bye, buddy," Seth says to him between sobs. Rachel and their blubbering boy cross the blacktop parking lot and disappear in through the security doors of the daycare. Seth doesn't see this, but he knows his wife is pushing her hand against the security scanner and waiting for the magnetic door to open. Like much of what they do as parents, this is a ritual that Seth believes will make his son safe.

Minutes later, enough for several other parents to come and go with their own children, Rachel returns and flops against the passenger seat in a puff. "He's quiet. Working on a puzzle." She announces this to the car, not necessarily to Seth.

Seth nods as he returns to the highway, pointing the car toward the gates of Mesa. His ride with Rachel is quieter now that Cody's out from the backseat, but now the tension's almost gone. He knows his wife is still angry at him, angry at what he did to their son, but it's just them now, and Seth feels freer to steal a glance at the v-neck cut in her scrubs along the way.

"I'll do it," he tells her. "I'll come to bed on time tonight." Seth stares over at the tan space between his wife's breasts and lingers on them. He holds the wheel as steady as he can without crashing.

"Good," she says. "This is serious." Rachel clears her throat and looks over to her husband. "Now eyes on the road, mister," she says, smirking almost imperceptibly, "or you'll kill us both."

At Mesa del Sol University, Assistant Professor Seth Baker works out the problem of the high inrush current on a new parabolic rig, but not in the way he thought he would. The projected sound beam is good and can run over 500 feet, but the power-up on the set has been ruining the first few seconds of recording. His new microphone, he reasons, will be the only thing that could listen past the initial thrum of electricity, and so only the Room itself can test whether or not the new specs are going to work.

Seth explains the problem to one of his research undergrads that morning: "Okay, say a LEO sees his target on the phone and needs to find out what he's saying and, more importantly, what the person on the other end is saying back. No time for a wiretap, and every second's precious, right? But if you need to record on a tactical, easy-to-use device that's going to give you solid amplification back, you lose the first few bits of recorded material because of that initial transient current. It sounds like mush and, of course, mushy recordings have difficulty getting turned into admissible evidence in court."

The undergrad nods, looks concerned but interested. "What's a LEO?"

"Law enforcement officer," replies Seth. "Saves time on distinguishing if they're a statie, officer, FBI agent, blah, blah, blah." There's a pause. The morning seems to drag on before him, and the undergrad's eyes keep drifting toward the entrance to the anechoic chamber.

"You've got homework this weekend," he tells the sophomore. "Go home and watch more cop shows. Pick up the lingo of whatever project you're working on. This is important for conference presentations."

Annoyed now, too, the undergrad excuses himself for the bathroom and stays in the lab next door for the rest of the morning, and this opens wide Seth's afternoon. There's time, then, to figure out the problem of the inrush current between approving the summer's research assistant candidate pool, but there's also time to test the new chamber now that the ribbon-cutting ceremony has been scheduled.

The late nights spent reviewing the Room's specs and construction process take Seth away from the sleep he needs to stop acting out his dreams. He and Rachel have visited physicians over this before, and the doctors can't quite trace out the pathway between the amount and type of sleep Seth needs and the levels of adenosine and cortisol in his system. All they've told him, then, is that he needs regular sleep and a watchful spouse, and when he's busy on the Room, Seth sees less of both of them.

It's finally finished, of course, but Seth can feel the need for precision eating chunks out of his available space and attention. Each night, Rachel somersaults unconsciously from comfortable pillow to comfortable pillow while waking to feed and change their son each time he cries out on the monitor, and it's important that Seth does his share. This means, then, learning how to work on a catch-22 sleep schedule that kills his REM.

He has to admit to himself, too, that he's no longer the young Physics major in the lab; he's the adult version of himself, the one who will feel the slow burn of age in his bones if he's not careful enough to rest them, but the Room, he knows, needs his attention if it's going to be functional.

When he rouses hours later on the lab couch, he's no more rested than before. The undergrad is long gone, but Seth discovers that someone has set up the parabolic microphone in the Room regardless. The monitors are on, the reflection plate has been laid out on the floor, the oscilloscope is running and recording, and even the lights are off so the mic can't pick up the burning filament in them.

While he slept, Seth realizes, someone had been testing the new rig. Someone had been using the Room, trespassing.

So Seth pads out in his loafers to the slate tiles of the hallway and listens. He checks his watch, sees that it is still early in the evening, and waits to hear the sound of a colleague or a visitor or a janitor. But there's nothing.

And there's nothing behind him but the still-running monitors of the Room and its harbored microphone. Nothing in front of Seth but the florescent bulbs and the long stretches of the research center.

Groggy and thirsty now, he stumbles over to the door of the Room itself and pulls on the great steel bar that hangs down its shining surface. He pulls open the reinforced metal of the quiet chamber and sees the back of the door that leads into the cage, a vault within a vault, and then he pushes its door open to reveal the smaller room and its prize.

"Was this me?" he asks no one, concerned he doesn't remember, but the Room eats his words.

To Seth, there's the feeling of entering a treasure room or the center of a technological labyrinth each time he swings open the plated doors. At other instances, as well, the Room is a torturer's cell, with its low-pressure system and its sharp lines and confining geometry, and it feels like this until he remembers that the steel doors can be opened easily from both sides.

It's silly to imagine that there would be someone waiting to electrocute him with the wire mesh that lines the floor and hangs above him, but this is how the Room was designed: four walls of meter-long polyurethane wedges that capture sound waves and absorb them without letting them reverb, bordered by a ceiling and a floor where the wedges hang above and below the wire mesh. Geometrically, the wedges look like teeth in the cold light of the bulbs. If a stranger were to wake up in the anechoic chamber, they'd imagine it was there as a torture device.

A colleague of his from the IT center had visited on Monday to marvel at it. "It's like a Farraday shield in here, isn't it?"

And Seth nodded. "It'll block most EM fields but not everything," he told his friend. "They've got those versions, sure, but this was expensive enough."

In this treasure room on this evening, then, Seth finds that his microphone's new settings are working, and that the device can record from the moment it's turned on to the moment it's turned off, free and clear and perfect. The moment does feel like a treasure, as well, since he has no idea how it's been delivered to him.

Seth once drove his family into downtown Las Cruces and could not remember how he got there. He and Rachel were on their way back from visiting her parents in El Paso, and the drive north to Santa Fe that once took four hours now took almost five at this stage in Rachel's pregnancy. The night before in the guest room was fitful for them both, but Rachel's parents were getting older and less likely to drive up on their own. So the young couple had instead resolved themselves to the misshapen bed at the back of the house. It was old and sagging, and, like great boulders drifting down into a valley, their bodies rolled toward each other when they moved and slept. In her expanding belly, as well, Cody's body somersaulted and fussed and kicked when he was pressed by anything outside of him and his mother.

So the couple left after a post-dinner nap that next evening. But as Rachel slept, Seth was instead kept awake by his in-laws' talk of plans for an upcoming cruise, and he busied himself by packing Rachel's gray Taurus with their suitcase and his wife's oversized pillow, the one that stretched the length of her growing body and the back seat. When she woke, they said their goodbyes and made plans to visit again, and they started north under the late stars of the desert.

Outside of Las Cruces, Seth's mind wandered from the sharp details of the new anechoic chamber at school into a ragged sleep, his eyes still open, though, like a shark's at rest, and the car veered from the straight line of I-10 onto the parallel of I-25.

Later, Seth would reason that it was his grogginess that almost killed his wife and their unborn son, and he resolved to pull over and sleep if he was ever too tired to go on in the future.

But late that night in New Mexico, something within Seth steered them toward a downtown intersection without giving him the memory of it. Under the desert clouds, under the space where lightning puffed out bright spots in the distance, Seth drove the Taurus on an autopilot setting his body seemed to flip over to when it was too exhausted for consciousness. His chassis of skin and muscle and bone signaled, changed lanes, slowed down the vehicle and sped it up as needed, and then the car came to a full stop at a red light and didn't move again for some time.

"Where are we?" Rachel asked. She had come to, leaning up now from her pillow stuffed against the passenger's window. The feeling of the road was different now, and something in her had sensed the ceasing of the push and pull of the drive north. She realized they were without velocity.

Seth blinked once and shook his head, unsure if he'd heard anything at all. If a hypnotist had mesmerized him, this was the snapping of fingers.

"I don't know," he said. There was a new but quiet panic in this, an alertness that hadn't been there before, then again: "I don't know."

At the intersection, below the red light that had then turned green, Seth and Rachel were alone and could see the closed shops around them and the light beaming out from the Bank of America sign. It read, "24 Hour ATM."

"Well, how did we get here?" asked Rachel. "You were driving."

Seth stepped out of the car and swiveled his head around. "I don't know. I just——." And that was all that could be said.

After a time, after the red light had gone green and back again twice, Rachel thought to ask, loudly this time in the intersection, "Were you asleep? Did you drift off?"

The switch of the autopilot fully off now, Seth admitted, "I don't know. I might have."

The lights clicked audibly and switched above them. "Jesus Christ, Seth!" Rachel fumed. "What if you plowed us into a pole or ramped us off an overpass? What the hell?"

And Seth apologized and apologized. He muttered these words in a chant that thrummed down into a whisper.

"I can drive," Rachel told him, not hearing his apologies anymore. "You need to sleep. So sleep." Sagging and tired in the heat still coming off from the ground, Seth watched his wife trudge to the driver's side door.

"Not a chance," he told her, revived. "We're both exhausted. Just let me sleep a bit and I'll be fine." It was Rachel's turn to swivel her head. Before them, in the distance, a red number glowed mutely.

"I need a bed, then," she told him. "Fifty bucks for a Motel 6 and the chance that we won't die on the road tonight is worth it."

So Seth agreed and let his wife drive them through two parking lots and down a cul de sac toward the bright motel in Las Cruces. While Rachel locked the doors and closed her eyes, Seth asked for a room, handed over his credit card, and then returned to his vehicle. He tapped softly on the window, and he watched his wife flip the lock on her side without opening her eyes.

Their drive home in the morning would be bright and cheerful again, and Cody would sleep in his mother's womb as they ripped up the highway so Seth could make it to his office hours at Mesa on time. But in the motel, after bringing in only the toiletry bags and his wife's body pillow from the car, Seth listened to Rachel's light breathing and the movement of gas and fluids in and through their bodies, and he wondered about the moment when he had blacked out on the highway and stopped the tape on his own memories that night.

Hours after returning home from his sleepwalker's test of the microphone in the chamber, Seth wakes to the sound of Cody wailing in his room down the hall, the noise amplified in the early morning by the transmission over the baby monitor on his night-stand, and he reminds himself that this is the biggest surprise in all his time so far as a parent. It wasn't the diminished sleep he'd go through for long stretches of weeks and months, and it wasn't the surprises that would fly out of his tiny son's digestive tract. Instead, it was the volume of the boy that he hadn't been prepared for, and he flinches most times he hears his son's banshee screams.

After coming into the world, Cody would wake up every two to three hours without explanation, and it drove Rachel and Seth into their own fits of exhausted panic. For the first eight months of Cody's life, as he breastfed, this would mean the quick snatch of their son from his bedroom into the kitchen, where a cool bottle of milk waited for him in the refrigerator. This was to be expected. But as the need for food in the night dropped off, Cody's lengths of time spent in sleep never did. Where Seth would take the first shift and listen for his son's cries from 10pm to 3am, the rest of the graveyard shift belonged to Rachel, the early riser in their family, and this would leave Seth to catch whatever scraps of sleep he could before work.

If Cody woke at night, there was always the mandatory change of his diaper, the attempt at rocking the boy back to sleep. If his son didn't pass out again, it would be time to take him down to the kitchen for food: a bottle of breast milk or a warmed cube of thawed apple sauce in the microwave that would contain a scoop of powdered oatmeal for more carbohydrates. If that didn't work, Seth would burp his son, pat him all over to release any trapped gases, and then try to get him back to slumbering one last time. If that didn't work, Seth took his son with him to their recliner, the place where Rachel had told him not to go with their child.

She'd heard a story from a client at work. The client had a friend whose child had died in its infancy, from asphyxiation. The friend's husband, she learned, worked swing shift. He came home and cared for his child after midnight, let his wife sleep as much as she could. In the morning, their roles reversed, and so he slept during the day while she made breakfast, took their baby to daycare, worked her own shift in the daylight. But no matter how he wanted to believe otherwise, the husband needed to reach an REM cycle during the night. On a particularly bad evening, three months after the wife had given birth, the husband fell asleep feeding their son in a recliner. When both father and son drifted off, they were warmed by the body heat of each other, they dreamed, and they were content. When the husband woke to his wife's screams of grief, he stared down into the worn space between his thigh and the interior of the La-Z-Boy, and he saw where his infant had slid during his watch, his open mouth against the upholstery, his body no longer moving.

Rachel came home heavy with that story. She made Seth promise not to fall asleep with Cody like that in the chair, and Seth avoided the comfort and the warmth of the recliner when he would feed their boy. To stay awake, he sat at the kitchen table, holding Cody and the bottles of warmed milk while staring at the rings on the varnish of the dark cherry wood. He thought of ways to stay awake at 1 and 2am, and he mostly did.

Tonight, Cody's burst of a scream shoots Rachel and Seth both awake, and Seth pats his wife's hip to tell her he's got this one. He switches off the monitor and shuffles down the hallway into the dark of his son's room, a faint blue from a nightlight glowing a path for him.

Cody is standing. He's grown and has accomplished this proudly, the ability to pull himself up by the wooden slats in his crib. He's learned to stand in the midnight hours, and he's learned this on his own, and Seth is proud of his son but knows that with more mobility comes more potential for harm. The scream, then, comes from a pedestal for volume, and it's loud and clear and constant.

"I'm here, buddy," Seth coos. "I'm here."

"Hrhm," huffs Cody. For reasons Seth doesn't understand, his son sobs until he holds him under each armpit and lifts.

Downstairs, the procedure's the same. A coffee cup of hot water goes into the microwave and warms. A bottle of breast milk gets dunked into the heat, and the cup is placed on the counter to warm. After a quick swig of orange juice from the fridge, straight from the carton, Seth walks with his son in circles around the living room until they're both more awake and the bottle can be chugged. Seth screws a nipple onto the bottle and looks dreamily over to the recliner he's not supposed to sit in right now.

At the kitchen table instead, Seth holds his son in his arms. Even when he eats, Cody is a loud child, and he gulps hungrily at the milk and pulls at the sleeves of Seth's robe. He inhales air and milk together, with volume, while his father stares out the window and waits for his son's screams when the first bottle empties.

In the morning, hours later, Rachel checks the nursery and finds nothing. She stumbles down the flight of carpeted stairs and looks next over at the easy chair in the living room. Nothing there, either. She listens for the sound of her husband and son, and then, hearing nothing but the compressor in their fridge, she starts to slip on her shoes to look for them again in the garage, not knowing what she'll find exactly.

Instead, there's Seth and Cody, the both of them in the kitchen now. She sees that Seth isn't holding their son. Rather, Rachel's husband is standing, soft and straight and tall, and when she looks around at his face, his eyes are open and half-lidded. He stares ahead, not down at the dark wood of the table in the kitchen nook where Cody snores on his back. There, in the center, Cody dozes, his head buoyed by the blanket Seth's wrapped him in, and there's Seth, the father of their child, looming over the table and staring straight ahead into something that's not quite there, into the warm distance of sunlight, not hearing Rachel's voice as she snaps her fingers and calls out his name.

The alarm goes off and brings morning into Seth's ears, and something's wrong. Something about his environment. He can tell. Without turning over to feel Rachel's legs against him, without listening for the hair dryer or the toilet or his own son's volume of babble from down the hall that comes with the daily act of just getting up, Seth knows the light in his room is brighter than it should be.

Somewhere outside of his first waking moments, his phone vibrates. A voicemail from his wife left more than an hour ago, and he's just now listening to it. His mouth is dry, and he can taste sour orange juice for some reason.

"Hi. First, don't worry about calling the lab. I told the student who picked up that you weren't feeling well and that you might not be in today, so please just sleep and take the day off. Second, you were sleepwalking—just standing—in the kitchen this morning, and you had Cody on the table, and he was about ready to fall off. He's fine, and I'm not mad. I'm just really concerned."

A pause. A chirp from Cody in the background as they drive to the daycare near campus.

"Actually, I am mad. I'm mad and I'm concerned, and I get to be both because this is our fucking son!"

To Cody: "Sorry, sweetie."

To her phone, to Seth: "I know you're busy and tired, but I also know you need to get your goddamn eight hours each night, or you're going to wind up hurting yourself. Badly."

Another breath. Deeper and more resolute now, almost a growl.

"Your work, your research, the promos and corporate requests: you can manage this during the day. From here on out, you either keep your work out of your mandatory eight hours of sleep each night, or you sleep on the lab couch until you get the full rest you need. Seriously, Seth." One last pause and then an added "Love you" before the click out.

He doesn't remember walking back upstairs from just a few hours ago, Rachel holding the small of his back and pushing him gently up onto the second floor of their home. He doesn't remember crawling back into bed and having the covers pulled up to his neck, and he doesn't remember Rachel's fingers as they brushed against his face and glided his eyelids down with them. He doesn't even remember the sound of the garage door opening, a feeling, a tremor that vibrates through the house and lets everyone know who's come home at that time.

Seth dials the lab, and the same student assistant picks up. "I'm fine," he tells him. "I'm just late. Going to catch the bus."

And he does. After a shower and coffee, he grabs his messenger bag and tries to remember where the neighborhood bus stop is in relation to their home on Greenbriar. In the distance, Seth hears the sound of jake breaks coming closer, and it's then that he remembers the bus stops two streets over on Terraza del Sol. Running now, Seth curses his wife and their shared car, and he waves his arms at the bus driver who pulls onto the street now and who waits for him.

Out of breath, Seth sits in an empty seat behind an elderly couple with sun visors. He holds his bag to his chest and stares up at the advertisements overhead: a real estate agency, a reminder to 'say something' if he 'sees something,' and a promo for Seton, an HVAC company that houses its corporate and manufacturing headquarters right here in Santa Fe. Their advertisement just mentions the name of the company and its blue and white glyph, as if anyone couldn't remember the name of one of the region's largest employers.

Seton, he remembers, was one of the first companies to put in a request for time with the Room. A rep with the company had driven over to Mesa to meet with him past the initial emails. His hair was dark and cropped short at the temples, and his light blue eyes were Rachel's eyes. They could have been cousins, and Seth warmed to him.

"We were planning to build one of these ourselves," the rep told him, "until we found out the university was getting its own. Model tests for volume and vibration don't happen that often, and it was going to be expensive as heck, you know?"

Seth did know. The tradeoff for the Room, he remembered, was that this was going to be his new life: meeting with corporate types, recommending ways to make their products quieter, filling in his own research in the meantime, of which there'd be little. Was this where the stress was coming from?

"You want to go in and check it out?" Seth asked the man, but the man shook his head and stepped back, smiling nervously. "Listen, the portable unit will definitely fit through the door. It's wide enough, I swear." But the Seton rep stayed in his corner, over near the couch.

"I've heard people go nuts from the lack of sound in chambers like this," he said. "How long do you have to be in there before it happens?"

This was always the question, the one that everyone wanted to know. Even the university president had asked him about it, and Seth had patted the man's shoulders and explained it to him, just as he explained it to the rep:

No, time spent in the room wouldn't drive you insane, although people did seem uncomfortable hearing their own heartbeats.

Yes, people could definitely spend longer than 45 minutes in anechoic chambers like Mesa del Sol's, unlike what the rumor was from that reporter.

Yes, you could hear your own blood pumping through your body, and, yes, you could hear yourself digest your lunch.

Seth wanted to ask the Seton rep if he'd heard of anyone who previously had hearing and who had then gone deaf go insane after the hearing loss. Did the elderly go nuts after their hearing loss accrued? No. Same thing with the anechoic chamber.

But this was what everyone wanted to know. Did the Room have the ability to change you? Yes, Seth wanted to say, but only if you were looking for peace and quiet and dark.

At Mesa, Seth hops off the bus and knifes over the cobblestones for the cool air of the lab and his equipment and the Room itself, and because he is behind on work and can't yet talk to Rachel, he stays late. He checks in with his assistant and asks about internships for the summer. He approves time in the Room for two more Seton projects and one for a kitchen appliance company that's closer to Albuquerque than it is to Santa Fe. He schedules a local TV crew to come in and film one of their field correspondents for a how-long-can-he-last-in-the-Room segment. Seth writes back, "He'll be bored. Tell him to bring a book."

Rachel calls just past 9:30 that evening. He's relieved and anxious about what she'll say. "I'm outside the lab and less angry now." She talks softly, so Cody must be in the car with her. "Cody woke up and was hungry, so I got him into his seat. Did you take a nap?"

Seth looks over to the lab couch, unused and with its two black pillows still propped up. "I did. I got some sleep. I'm still tired, but I got some sleep."

Cody starts to cry in the background. "Good," Rachel says, putting the car in gear again. "Hop in outside, and we'll go to bed."

At home, Seth yawns in between bites of a PBJ on wheat toast. He pads up the steps when he can't hear his son's cries anymore and passes out in bed without brushing his teeth, without waiting for his wife to slip in next to him.

He wakes to the sound of his son's warm breath coming from behind him. Above him, dim light from a bulb hits him in the face like a ray gun, and, in between Cody's gasps for air, Seth feels his boy's short breaths as they stream over the back of his neck. They come at him like a roaring piston from below where he's sitting upright, from where Cody's small hands paw at him and squeeze his shirt like paper, clenching and releasing and gripping again. In this small box, he is assailed by sound.

In the Room, although Cody isn't crying, he is the loudest thing Seth has ever heard.

He looks down at his watch and sees that it is morning, just after seven. He can hear the ticking of the second hand, feels it vibrate on his skin like ants marching. Seth knows this, but this and the volume of his son, who claws at him now like someone drowning, are the only things he knows for certain.

Below where his drool and his tears have rivered together, Cody's chest bumps up against Seth's arm. He rests against the foam pads of the diffusing wedges in the chamber, crushing them, where each brush against the material runs out like white rapids of volume. In the dim light, though, Seth watches his son open his mouth to scream and cry, but nothing bursts from him. How long has he been like this? How long has it taken him to fear the sounds coming from his own body?

In between silent sobs where Cody's mouth opens to reveal nothing but black and wet in the dark room, his son flinches against the sound of his own blood thrumming through his ears, and this is where Cody plants his hands at his temples as he cries silently. Seth doesn't know how many hours he's been asleep in the Room, crouched and leaning up against the walls of the anechoic cube, but he knows this is the first time he's brought a passenger with him in the nighttime.

In his pocket now, his phone vibrates like a tornado warning, and Cody jumps back from the din and the volume. In the dim light of the Room, Seth sees it is Rachel calling, her name flashing across the screen, and he knows what must have happened in a measure of car keys, a drive across town, the closing of heavy vaulted doors behind the bodies of himself and his child. He presses the button to talk and, in the silence of the chamber, the cries of his wife fill it like an ocean pouring into a thimble.

"Where are you?" she screams. "Where is my son?"

Ghosts Caught on Film

In the length of time it takes you to affix the image of a woman's ribcage to a sheet of gel-colloid film, you remember three things. First, today is a Wednesday, overcast and snowy outside. Second, the woman's name is Jill. She works at a tanning salon. Third, our names for the days of the week stem from Nordic tradition, from homage paid to Odin on Wednesdays, Thor on Thursdays, Frea the next.

"I wipe up semen in the booths at work," she replies. "But I'm training to be a massage therapist."

You press a button. Viciously fast electrons now bore through a body.

"Wait. What do you do at the salon?" you ask, curious now because maybe you didn't hear something accurately but also because you're being polite. The questions you ask keep the patients you shoot at the hospital preoccupied. You remember this is a good thing.

But you remember lots of other things, too, though only after the x-rays have passed through Jill's thick frame of muscle and bone and body fat that must be in there somewhere: that the hippocampus, tiny nub of tissue that it is, is the director of memory in the brain; that the bridge between the two hemispheres is called the corpus callosum; that graphite in pencil lead is a crystalline structure of repeating carbon.

"Jake," she whispers. But it seems so loud in this room. "I clean up jizz. It's disgusting."

"We have to do a lateral now," you say. "I know it's cold. I'll be quick."

You remember that 'jizz' is a variation of 'jism.' It used to mean one's energy or spirit. It now means one's semen.

"Jake?"

Most rooms that house radiology equipment are cold. You're not sure why, and this lack of information kicks at you in these quiet, alone times in the staff break room. CTs, PETs, MRIs, ultrasounds, x-rays: each machine is forever stored in cold, refrigerator-like rooms.

You clear your throat and recall that phlegm and mucous are sticky fluids the body creates so as to trap foreign and unwanted bacteria.

"I need you to turn 90-degrees to the left," you say. "There, Jill. That's it. Now stick your arms out in front, take a deep breath, and hold."

Jill turns, revealing an ornately built flow of muscle from deltoid to bicep and triceps, to radialis and ulnaris. You're staring. She fills her lungs with air, corks her own trachea in hopes that she won't have to return to this hospital for another year, you believe. Her arms hefted in front of her give her the look of a golem.

You turn dials with markings of fractions and guideposts of time. You measure radiation here and how fast it will amplify through Jill's gargantuan arms as it flows towards her chest.

"People masturbate in the booths," she spills through her teeth, her arms still stocked. "They get bored, you know?"

You press a button the color of overripe limes. A surge of measured kilovolts-per-second travels through the ballast, heating a coil of superheated tungsten that spits out radiation in a series of equally measured amps and waves, all penetrable, all galloping instantaneously across the room to a cancer-survivor's chilled torso. The wave particles that bounce off the silver-based exposures in the film cassette try their very best to hit you, as well. But there's double-paned glass and a wall protecting you, both lined with resistant lead.

"You should come in for a haircut sometime," she whispers. "I think I can get you a discount on styling gel."

You know these things. This knowledge, like the lead between you and the cathode tube, keeps you clean.

On your first day here at St. Bartholomew's, they reminded you about the time clock and the importance of being present at the beginning of your shift. They gave you a clearance badge. They winked at you and told you that the cafeteria food was both bland and overpriced, and that there was a café across the street that made box lunches wrapped in both foil and a greasy love for health professionals.

And they told you about the massive patient charts. Each division is never singularly functional. Each compartment's information requires additional information from the other compartments in the patient's chart. Before a physician can plan out a regimen of chemotherapy, you know, she must consult the PET scan in the imagery compartment, the tumor markers from lab work, and the cell type of the adenocarcinoma from pathology. Medical information gels together to create a metaphysical patient, a conglomerate and imaginary body upon which one may work.

And here is the body of Jill Cleburn, virtual and documented.

A date of birth. A family history of diabetes but not carcinoma. A pathology report of the estrogen and progesterone receptors, both negative, both beneficial given her history. A list of medications and supplements: echinacea, vitamin E, selenium, Femara.

You turn pages.

Physician's notes: "Jill Cleburn," you read, "is a 23-year old female with a history of Breast CA. She presents today for her first annual follow-up. Patient successfully completed excision of 3-centimeter tumor from the left breast over a year ago, subsequent radiation therapy, and two cycles of Tamoxifen. A switch to Femara was recommended this last June pending Miss Cleburn's request for a lower dose of hormones. ER/PR negative. Today's chest x-ray reveals shading now in the right breast. Will schedule patient for a repeat series to be shot within 48 hours immediately. If shading persists, schedule a chest CT. Follow-up in one week." And physicians always sign off with their names.

This shading, Jake? You have to see this for yourself.

Down in the dark of the radiology library, pegged up and steadied against the bright and burning lights of the fluorescent displays, there is the draped film of emission artistry.

In the two years you've been employed at St. Bartholomew's, you have come to appreciate the human body for its hidden structure, for those blocks of bone that make skin jut out at crests and joints. You feel privileged in some ways to be able to see these things that most can't.

Jill Cleburn's body is up on the wall. Her date of birth again. Her patient number. Her structure.

In the soft blue light of the display, the first things you see are the ribs. They seem almost coiled towards the spine, all of them forming a loop between the sternum and the vertebrae behind it. You see the quick spirals of clavicles, the stump of a humerus, the faint whispers of the heart and lungs and the blood vessels that stream between them.

And then you see it. In the black and the white and the blue and the gray of Jill's frame, you see the shading mentioned in the physician's note. Near the end of the drop of Jill's right breast, in the ghost image of a woman's chest, you see the bloom of a webbing, white and dangerous. It perches ephemerally next to a clump of thin bronchioles. It waves at you in the dark of the library.

On the short walk home from the hospital each night—five blocks south, two west—you feel the privilege of slow travel and neighborhood-grade concrete. Each window you pass informs you about the people behind it: the concerned look certain fathers get on the phone, even when talking to friends. The way children can stare at a television and hold entire conversations divorced from the trajectories of their own eyes. The concentration of women. Between late March and mid-October, you step down the hill from St. Bartholomew's to your quiet three-bedroom, one-and-a-half-bath near the bulge of a cul de sac. The grass on the lawn, you remember, has slowed its growth because of the cool air that has started to thicken each morning, and this is fine because it means less mowing and that it's time to plant tulip bulbs and iris. Inside, your bedroom is logged with cases and shelves of books—biographies of engineers and architects, professional reference tomes, contemporary British fiction—enough so that they spill into the office across the carpeted hallway. The guest room, you remember, houses both an extra bed and, company not present, a soft pallet for warm, clean laundry.

You remember there is a flank of salmon in the refrigerator with paprika and ground pepper that needs to be grilled. Oranges and grapefruit sit next to a red onion on the bottom shelf. The tiles on the kitchen floor are cold to the skin on the bottom of your feet, but, for some reason, you remember that the easiest way to keep your extremities warm is to wear a cap; if the most vital organ, the brain, has enough heat being delivered, the body will find ways of directing warm blood elsewhere. You know this process is called 'vasodilation,' and that, when this action is sudden, skin flushes and reddens quickly. Blood vessels widen when the smooth muscle tissue in the surrounding wall is relaxed. And you know that these tiny floods below the skin can occur when the body is removed from a cold environment to a warmer one.

"I've never tanned before," you reply.

Jill is dressed in her work uniform: a white polo shirt with the name of the spa, Les Belles, stitched onto the front pocket, khaki pants, sneakers, makeup. She hands you a towel, and you wonder if the hospital has called her back for her radiology appointment.

"Your haircut looks nice," she says. You think she means this.

"Thanks," you say. "The woman in that red smock did it." Jill looks over into the salon chairs of Les Belles, recognizes someone and waves. "Should I have tipped up here at the desk instead?" You remember that "Les Belles" is French for "the beautiful ones."

This pleases you.

"I have to ask," she says, whispering, leading you down a small hallway lined with particle-wood doors in white. The doors are numbered in gold. "Didn't they tell you about the radiation from these things? Don't you get enough at work?"

You know that Wilhelm Conrad Roentgen discovered x-rays in 1895. You know that the measured unit of radiation is named for Roentgen. You know that radiologists have the shortest life span of all physicians, but you're not sure about the demographics for technicians like yourself. This missing fact cuts at you.

"You got me interested," you say. "I consider this research almost."

Jill Cleburn now stops and turns towards you. You believe that she is sizing you up, that she is wondering what kind of person you are, seeing as you have come to the place where she works and cleans up semen for a living. But she smiles and keeps walking.

"Here's number eight," Jill says. She hands you a pair of plastic cups that fit snugly over your eyes. "These are little sunglasses. Don't look too closely at the bulbs in the booth without them."

The room, ten feet by eight, houses a white metal booth—the "Baja 985"—and a small table and chair set. There are pegs on the door for your clothes.

"I'll see you in twenty minutes," Jill chirps before she leaves.

It feels strange, you believe, to be naked down to one's briefs while in front of large, glowing machinery.

In the booth, you feel heat. You nod off because it has been a long day at St. Bart's and because you are warm and in your underwear. In between thoughts of caustic electrons ripping apart the RNA in your sebaceous glands, you dream of your own patient history and what you might read about yourself if a file were created just for you.

Do they make medications for this? you wonder.

This is your history: birth, snaps of neural connections, kindergarten, sandboxes, sandwiches, the substitute in seventh grade, the YUMberland drive-through girl, diploma, certification, the hospital. The radiology unit at St. Bartholomew's. Each time you look at a mirror, each time you accidentally look into the deep hollows of your own eyes—you search for looming acne, mostly—you run through this list. But you can never really hammer down the specifics of each item.

Something clicks from within the booth.

No one remembers their own birth. No one has a mind developed enough for this task. This is where the neurons come in. You know that your brain had to build neural pathways so you could hold your head up for five seconds, or so you could close your lips together to suck in strained beets. You know that you needed thousands of connections just so you could utter your first paired syllables—"ma ma"—with the masseter muscles in your jaw.

You can hear a samba playing on the P.A. system from outside of the glowing lights. You can smell the sweat from your own left armpit.

There had been playgrounds and bologna and cheddar on wheat. And then there was the curled hair of the woman who subbed your pre-algebra class in seventh grade. You don't remember her face, just the fountain of auburn curls and the fact that hair twists like that because the proteins swoop down in alpha-helices. And the nineteen-year old with her G.E.D. who licked her lips at you each time you pulled up for a medium-rare YUMburger with YUMustard. The pile of socks back at her apartment stank of fries, but her breath—you remember this—poured all over your neck like peppermint oil.

So this is what you remember each time you get a sideways glance into a reflective surface? Yes. But now you wonder about Jill, pose questions to yourself about her, answer them all in kind.

Did she graduate from high school like you did? Most likely. Did she need certification to clean up sperm deposits at the spa? Probably not, but you wonder what she knows of proper HAZMAT technique.

At the end of twenty minutes, after you pay for just a haircut—"The tan's complimentary," she says, smiling. "You shoot me, I shoot you"—Jill Cleburn hands you a bottle of green lotion and tells you to rub this on the exposed skin sometime tonight before you go to bed. You say goodbye and are somehow able to avoid a "See you soon!" because you remember that you will most likely be the one to take radiographs of her chest again in the next two days.

Outside, you remember that the aloe vera plant is native to South America, that it belongs to the Liliaceae family. Snow collects quietly on the concrete.

Is it perhaps because you're admiring the glow of the television light on her rippled forearms that you're standing outside of her window in the falling flakes of snow, your socks too far down in your pants that the white crystals of ice are actually melting into your shoes, your jacket just a bit too thin for this type of cold weather, your head uncovered and gathering thin flakes as much as you are on your shoulders?

Or is this something else, Jake?

Skin still flushed and warm from the blue rays of the tanning booth, you're here at her house now, freezing, watching her drink yellow-tinged juice from a high-density polyethylene carton. You know that this type of plastic is easy to melt and recycle. And Jill Cleburn's cinnamon hair and marbled eyes and gauze-white skin all glow blue in the light of the news in pictures onscreen: a financial analysis of what looks like the weak orange crop this year, a burning streak in popularity for an aging singer/songwriter, nuclear facility failures in the Mekong delta.

You watch her and know that a television's vacuum picture tube emits red, green, and blue ultraviolet-light electrons from within a cathode; that a television screen is coated with phosphor so it can glow when bombarded by this light; that what we see on the screen is the proud burning of this phosphor each time an electron crashes into it just so.

And in the glow of the phosphor, Jill Cleburn burns just as brightly, and a patch of white within her chest lights up the pitch dark surrounding it. You remember this luminescent webbing and hope that the hospital won't wake Jill up tomorrow morning too early when they call, if they haven't already.

You remember here, Jake, staring through the window in the cold, that double-paned glass helps to prevents heat from escaping.

It's only when you see her put down the juice and pick up a wooden dowel the size of a handlebar that you realize you are shivering and that your areolae have become little calluses that poke against the cotton of your shirt. You follow the trace of a string attached to the middle of the foot-long dowel down to the floor, to a brick by her feet.

You watch Jill Cleburn against the moving flickers of Somalian children toting voluminous M60s as the cancer-survivor begins to grip and curl the wooden baton in her hands. She winds her wrists and pulls the dowel on the contraption, and the string grows taut; you witness the brick lift from the floor in staccato, jerky motions. While you watch the systolic pump of her arms' extensors and flexors, a new sedan is unveiled on the screen. Two announcers appear to exchange banter and perfect-white smiles. An elderly man and woman ride bicycles on a hillside before a diamond-shaped pill appears at the bottom left corner of the television.

And then you see Jill Cleburn cry. But her lips don't purse. But she doesn't blubber. But her face doesn't contort. Instead, her eyes just pour tears now in front of a televised commercial: two women in sunlit door frames, hair all loose and blowing and feather light, both in brassieres and their underwear. You watch as the camera cuts to a close-up of a new one-step clasp, nestled between two globes of tanned, soft skin.

"'Shading' is when an area on your film shows up that isn't clearly identifiable," you reply. "It's a superstition on the radiograph, like a ghost caught on film."

Jill Cleburn stands sluggishly at the back of the poorly lit x-ray room. Her back touches a composite plate that hides a cassette of undeveloped film. She wears a thin apron of cloth for a top. The rest of her—jeans and leather sandals—is clothed normally below the belt line.

"These tops don't leave much to the imagination, do they?" she asks. There is gooseflesh at her wrist.

"Sorry it's so cold in here again," you say. "I think they keep it at this temperature to give the technicians a thrill." She smiles at this. She smiles and beams perfect-white teeth towards your eyes.

"We have to shoot a series before we can make the ghost start to disappear," you say.

She nods, looks now towards the wall at her left.

"I lost most of my hair last time," she says. In the dim light of this room in the radiology unit, you know that Jill Cleburn is talking about her previous dance with metastatic cells that divided and spread across her frame. "After chemo," she whispers, "it came back this color."

Cinnamon. You know that the bark of the cinnamon tree evolved as a means to keep predatory insects away. This information keeps you focused.

"I used to be a brunette with curls," she says.

You begin with a right lateral shot. The cassette behind the metal frame she is standing in front of is already loaded and clipped with undeveloped film. Pointing now towards the exit sign, Jill's arms extend out again like a springboard diver's. You watch her in her concentration through the lead-lined glass. You press a button down against a metal station of dials and knobs, and electrons ricochet away from her like small kernels you just can't see.

You change out the cassettes. Being so close to her in the process, you know her hair smells of pomegranate and peach.

"Did I tell you I like your haircut?" she asks.

"Look towards the tube," you say.

"Breathe in and hold it," you say.

In the booth again, you reset the kilovolts and the amps. You transfer the measured width of her body now to the movements of two dials, and now you press a button.

This is a microwave running with the door open, a television projecting with the screen popped off: beams and waves and particles fly through Jill Cleburn's body in heated anger.

Replacing one cassette for another again, you wonder about the webbing of light you first saw just days ago. You remember how you felt so abashed that you caught it in motion and in the chest of a woman so young.

"Look towards the wall for me, okay?" you say. You watch her turn to the left.

And you know that seeing the patch of white again today means that Jill will have a CT scan scheduled. And you know that the scan, if it comes to that, will reveal a webbing of metastases, of a host of hidden cells somewhere in her right breast.

Back in the booth, you watch the ripples of muscle that cord Jill's back and shoulders. She is staring down at her chest, and this makes her neck bulk out into lumps of muscle. You know these are called the trapezii, named after their resemblance to the geometric figure. Outside in the hallway, you hear a physician being paged.

"I'm trying my very best to make it disappear," you say.

You press a button.

Acknowledgments

There are so, so many people I need to thank, and I'm worried about forgetting anyone, and about not knowing how to thank all the names on this list properly. I'll start these acknowledgements, then, by stating flat out that I will never, ever be able to pay these wonderful people back adequately for their kindness.

To Caleb Michael Sarvis and the rest of the team at Bridge Eight Press, who have taken a hell of a chance on publishing my story collection. Their hard work in building such a humdinger of a press is forever appreciated, and I can't thank them enough for promoting their authors' works.

To the literary magazine editors I've worked with over the years who published earlier versions of these stories, please know how much I've appreciated your acceptances and your critiques: Roxane Gay, Kevin Allardice, Aimee Pokwatka, Vicki Lawrence, Janell Watson, Barb Johnson & Kailyn McCord & MM Kaufman, Juli Min, Nicholas Gilmore, Lydia Munnell & Abigail Cloud, David Lazar, M.E. Parker & Shane Oshetski, and Heather Bartlett. Your late-night emails of encouragement have reminded me that maybe, just maybe, I don't suck at this.

To David James Poissant, for choosing "Hands Like Birds on

Strings" for Bayou Magazine's James Knudsen Prize, and, years later, for the excellent advice on how to put a story collection together. When someone whose work you love says they love your work, it's a hell of a confidence boost.

To my creative writing teachers, I'm forever thankful for your patience and your encouragement to get weird: Jaimee Wriston Colbert, Molly Giles, Donald 'Skip' Hays, Susan Jackson Rodgers, Joanne Meschery, Imad Rahman, and John 'Jack' Vernon. I've learned at your tables and have come away better for the time I spent in your company.

To the early readers of these stories who sat with me in workshops and writing groups, and whose comments made my work immeasurably better: Natalia Andrievskikh, Matthew Burns, Lincoln Carpenter, Christie Grimes, Kathryn Henion, Gray Hilmerson, Jason Kirker, Christopher Myers, Jennifer Pashley, Kristen Cox Roby, José Rodriguez, Virginia Shank, Joe Szewczyk, Kim Vose, Matthew Webber, Holly Wendt, and Todd Wright, and so many others who have made these drafts into actual stories.

To Aggeliki Pelekidis, who for years was a constant reader and editor, and who served as a reminder that it's important to stop and enjoy the work itself sometimes, you know?

To Jason Allen, my Zhōngguó Xiōngdì, who's forever been an incredible source of inspiration. I look forward to every, single conversation we'll ever have with each other.

To my brother, Ryan Bowlin, for keeping me grounded and for being an outstanding uncle. I love you, you complete bastard.

To my parents, Brenda and Philip Bowlin, for the decades of unabashed love and support and encouragement, and for never once trying to dissuade me from being an English major. I had a wonderful childhood, and I know I'm incredibly lucky.

To my children, Sierra and Cormac, for letting me steal moments from your lives to use in my work.

And to my wife, Cari. You've given me your love and your time and your patience and the space to write, and I can't wait to grow old and haggard with you.

www.ingramcontent.com/pod-product-compliance
Lightning Source LLC
Chambersburg PA
CBHW021134190726
48288CB00008B/2652